All rights reserved, no part of this publication may be reproduced or transmitted by any means whatsoever without the prior permission of the publisher.

Text © Diane Narraway

Front cover created using public domain images modified by Diane Narraway.

Edited by Veneficia Publications and Fi Woods

October 2022

Typesetting © Veneficia Publications UK

VENEFICIA PUBLICATIONS UK

veneficiapublications.com

Devolution

Book 1: Exodus

Diane Narraway

Somewhere between Science and religion lies the truth

FOR MY CHILDREN

CONTENTS

CHAPTER 1	1
CHAPTER 2	3
CHAPTER 3	13
CHAPTER 4	28
CHAPTER 5	41
CHAPTER 6	61
CHAPTER 7	79
CHAPTER 8	105
CHAPTER 9	112

CHAPTER 10	117
CHAPTER 11	142
CHAPTER 12	156
CHAPTER 13	174
CHAPTER 14	182
CHAPTER 15	194
CHAPTER 16	198
CHAPTER 17	208
CHAPTER 18	213
CHAPTER 19	229

PROLOGUE

Towards the turn of every century prophecies foretelling the end of the world and the destruction of humankind are equally as prevalent as man-kind's hope for a better future.

The end of the twentieth century was no exception, seeing translations of the Biblical prophecies foretold in the Revelation of St. John rise to epic proportions. Largely because at the turn of a millennium, everything becomes more climactic.

Everything from asteroids to alien invasion. Everybody with an ex-tinction-level theory wanted to share it, aided, and abetted by the media and Hollywood. There couldn't have been anyone alive in the western world who hadn't heard of Armageddon or the Anti-Christ or didn't know at least one quotation from the last book of the Bible.

Nevertheless, despite all the hype, it didn't happen.

There was no second coming (or at least, not as far as anyone knew), there was no 'Rapture' and there was no Anti-Christ, although there were a few good candidates.

There were no 'Four Horsemen', just the usual deaths, viruses, famines, and wars, which had been happening since the beginning of time.

There was no Armageddon, a word translated from 'Har Megiddô,' a Hebrew phrase implying a meeting upon a hill or mountain. In the case of the biblical Armageddon, it was the place where God puts an end to the kingdoms and governments of the Earth, (although it was occasionally translated by conspiracy theorists as the United Nations). There was no resurrection of the dead—in fact, there was no real sign of a biblical apocalypse at all.

By 2001 both the Earth and humanity were still in place, which for many may well have been a disappointment.

The first few years saw science progress both on, and off the Earth. There were also a few religious shake-ups, which came with man's new age of discovery. Medicine had made several major breakthroughs, which not only allowed people to live a bit longer but improved the quality of old age.

By 2043 it was legal in most countries to clone human embryos and as a result they were successfully used to cure several degenerative dis-eases including Parkinson's disease, Alzheimer's disease, strokes, cancer, leukaemia, HIV, and diabetes. Stem cells had become household words, whereas a few years earlier those same words sent human rights campaigners on a rampaging moral crusade. It's strange how ideas can change when it becomes not only beneficial to people but affordable.

With the change in moral attitudes towards the cloning of human embryos, the 'designer baby' market found its niche. Although this was considered unethical by many, without question there was a demand for beautiful, clever, and above all, healthy babies. This meant sperm banks paid a fortune for men with the 'right qualifications: good looks, intelligence, physique etc.. Likewise female egg donors, which put the cost of having a 'designer baby' anywhere from £5,000,000–£20,000,000+. The price depended on how many designer attributes such as eye colour, hair colour, and IQ were required, and of course the location of the clinic.

Organ transplant was another area where significant breakthroughs were being made, although due to many other advances in medicine trans-plants were becoming less necessary. In many transplant cases, animal organs (usually pigs) had replaced human ones and due to better immune-suppressive drugs, the newly transplanted organs were not so easily reject-ed by the body. Even though pigs' valves had been used in heart surgery since the 1960's, this was still new territory. Sadly, the lack of education on animal to human transplants meant the black market still continued to supply human organs to those who feared the media translation of a 'possible virus mutation, caused by animal–human organ replacement. To date, no virus had however occurred.

'Orexin' too had become a household name and was sold in chemists and pharmacies around the world. As a natural stimulant derived from neurons located in the hypothalamus, it was initially used to treat disorders such as narcolepsy and M.E. but had later become used for military 'night operations.' It eventually found its way into society, where it was instantly popular with shift workers and teenagers at all night parties; with no side effects it was a safe replacement for caffeine and the synthetic amphetamines sold on the streets.

N.A.S.A. too had its own records of achievement, which later included the discovery of a new planet in our solar system. A more distant, icy, but larger in mass planet than the reclassified dwarf planet Pluto and, more importantly, one that met all the criteria to be classified as a planet and not just a member of the Kuiper Belt. This would remain un-named for reasons that were never clear or obvious.

Another project was the launch of a probe sent out to explore what lies beyond our solar system. It was intended that the information would be accessible to future generations, although it is probable that by the time it completes its mission future generations would probably be able to get there faster themselves.

The big early 21st Century project and, by far the greatest achievement, was the *crewed* mission to Mars. The astronauts left Earth in September 2038 and returned four years later with their discoveries posing nearly as many questions as they answered. They did, however, answer some. Not only was there water on Mars but there is water on Mars. The frozen polar caps appeared to be made of water and although they did not manage to drill deep enough to find any in liquid form, the ice samples they brought back, once melted were indeed water.

The Vatican too were moving their goalposts left, right, and centre, as were many other Christian denominations. Firstly, there had been no end of the world to be saved from, which meant not only might their book be wrong but worse still, it meant less power and less control over the minds of its followers. Secondly, for the first time in well over a millennia most of Europe had stopped paying taxes to the Vatican, reasoning they didn't need to be saved from something that hadn't and probably wouldn't happen; the potential for life having existed on Mars meant that man may not be the only thing created in God's image. This all came alongside demands that the Vatican reveal its hidden knowledge and share the scrolls that it had kept secret for almost 2000 years.

  Needless to say, the Vatican side stepped, backtracked and did just about every dance possible, kicking and screaming all the way but never giving in.
As for the rest of life—well, that was the same as ever: people weren't super-fit immortal beings looking like they'd stepped off the cover of the latest girlie or action magazine. Nor was everyone wearing silver cat-suits. They looked and dressed the same as they had for the last 40 years or more. If anything, the majority were more obese and unfit than the previous generation, relying on new medical advances to cure any diseases or problems they inflicted upon themselves.

Fast food, alcohol, cigarettes, and certain fizzy drinks were still as popular as ever, despite the numerous 'get healthy or die horribly' campaigns. And in any major town or city the homeless, whose only friend is drugs or alcohol, still littered the streets and doorways.

This was the world by 2045 and there was no one who was prepared for what was to come.

CHAPTER 1

For the first time ever in his life, he felt a deep, calm inner peace. He breathed in deeply, aware of the fragrant sedative that, although only faint now, he knew from past experience would soon become overpowering.

"This is it then?"

His host smiled back at him.

"Yes, my friend. This is it."

It was always the same response. Calm, honest, and accompanied by a reassuring smile, behind which lay a wisdom that was as old as time itself. Despite all he had learned over the last few hours, he knew nothing compared to this man with a Mona Lisa smile. As the scent slowly filled the room, he reflected over the last ten years, trying to catalogue the chain of events that had finally brought him to this place.

If he had been a writer, he felt sure that his story would have been worth telling. It may not have been totally believable, but it would most definitely have been interesting. He traced back through all that he had been shown to find the point where, for him, it had all begun. Technically, it should have started with his birth, but for the first fifty years or so his life had been much like anybody else's. The events leading up to this moment had their roots laid down much later in his life.

He had been shown so much in the last few hours that it was becoming increasingly difficult for him to remember anything with any clarity. The sedative wasn't making it any easier for him either. Drifting slowly into unconsciousness, his hazy memories were replaced by a primordial void where everything and nothing co-exist in infinity. Buried deep within that void were the events that led him there: events that began a little over ten years ago, with a letter he had received on 25th October 2045.

CHAPTER 2

"Not another one?" she quizzed, looking over her glasses with raised eyebrows. It was a concerned look as much as a question; anyway, the look on President Gerry Mcquillan's face said far more to her than his actual words.

"I'm afraid so," he replied slowly.

"It's the fifteenth this month." She had worked with him long enough to know that he was disturbed by this.

"I don't know Jen … These people are really starting to bug me." His voice almost revealed a self-confession of concern as he handed her the letter.

Gerry McQuillan had come into office in 2042 and had always been more than just a figurehead. He had stated during his presidential campaign that he intended to 'Make a difference to the quality of every American citizen's way of life,' and that is exactly what he strove to do. He was a tall, somewhat delicate man with slightly greying hair that gave his appearance its 'dignified look'. He spoke with an air of compassionate authority, which demanded that people listen to him. But now, he was concerned; 'This letter' was clearly bothering him.

Jenny was not only his Secretary of State: she was also his friend. She had been with him ever since she graduated from college, and was originally employed as his secretary, later becoming his personal assistant working alongside him and his wife throughout the Presidential campaign. She had worked hard, and not only was she one of the few women ever to become Secretary of State, but at twenty-six she was also the youngest person ever to hold office. Jenny was always the one Gerry McQuillan confided in when his wife was either unavailable, unauthorised, or when he simply didn't want to worry her. She read through the letter:

'Dear Mr President,

I am writing once again to stress the urgency of action needed in the Yellowstone National Park region.

Seismic activity in that area suggests we may be only weeks, if not just days, away from a volcanic eruption of Biblical proportions. Evacuation of the 650-mile radius, which we estimate to be in danger, should have begun days ago, with emergency aid and shelter already in place.

I can only assume that you are choosing not to take this seriously, as we are not a large government-funded establishment and therefore do not warrant either respect or credibility. I urge you to rethink, and for the sake of humanity take the necessary action immediately.

Yours faithfully,

P. Scott

Yellowstone Development Consultancy'

Jenny handed the letter back, looked thoughtful, sucked in air, and added, "They really wanna put the pressure on, don't they? I'll see what 'Our People' have got." With that, she turned to leave, with a look of unrivalled determination and efficiency that any pioneer would be proud of.
"Thanks, Jen." She softened and smiled as she left the room.
Gerry read through the letter again. As he had never heard of 'Yellowstone Development Consultancy' before these letters started, he had originally considered the possibility of it being a terrorist plot. He wasn't entirely sure exactly what they would hope to achieve by a mass evacuation. Whilst it would be costly, it wouldn't really do any significant damage to the economy. He did know

better now: at least now he knew they were a real company. However, he seriously hoped these people were wrong, better still, they were just a bunch of nut cases trying to gain a modicum of notoriety. Hopefully, Jenny would come up with something more positive.

"Morning Charlotte," Jenny smiled at her personal secretary. She believed everyone should be greeted first, before any other requests were made of them and, apart from anything else, she genuinely liked Charlotte who, despite the horrific red lipstick, which always made her look like she was ready for a good night in, and dark curly hair, reminded her of herself.

"Good morning, Ma'am."

"Charlotte, can you get the Yellowstone Geological Centre on the phone please?"

"OK Ma'am; no problem."

Normally Jenny hated the words 'no problem'. Usually, they meant there was at least one, if not several, problems, but today they were the right words to hear. At least something wasn't a problem. She sat at her desk, leant back in the chair, and wondered what would happen if they were right? What if a 650-mile radius did need to be evacuated? It just wasn't possible that something like that could happen. Not now. Not in 21st century America. No.

They couldn't be right, and that was that! The phone ringing dragged her out of her morbid speculation.

"Got Yellowstone for you, Ma'am."

"Thank you, Charlotte ... Hello?"

"Well, well. If it isn't our illustrious Secretary of State ... So, how have you been, Jen? It's been a while."

"Fergus?"

This couldn't be happening. The arrogant voice at the other end of the phone was, without any shadow of a doubt, Fergus Moreno. An ex-boyfriend from her distant past: Irish on his mother's side and Puerto Rican on his father's. Easy to fall in love with and just as easy to hate. Good looking, incredibly intelligent, and about the most patronising, arrogant, and self-centred man she had ever known.

"You remember me ... I'm flattered."

"Well don't be! This is serious. Do you think we can save your trip down memory lane for another time?"

"I suppose so. Just what particular crisis is the White House having today?"

"Have you ever heard of Yellowstone Development Consultancy?"

"Doomsday Peg ... Sure have." He couldn't help laughing.

"Yeah, okay. What's so funny?"

"More than anything, that your

phoning me has anything to do with Peggy Scott."

Jenny was finding it increasingly infuriating listening to Fergus sniggering.

"Please, Fergus ... this is important."

"Christ, Jen ... You're serious, aren't you?"

"Yes, I am!" she snapped. "Now can you please tell me what you know?"

"Okay, look ... Peggy was a lecturer at the university when I was a student. She's a colourful character."

"What exactly does that mean?"

"Well, rumour was that she had to leave the university ... she'd never admit that though. Anyway, the rumour was that she'd been having an affair with another married professor. I say 'another' because it wasn't the first time; she had a bit of a wild reputation."

"What else?"

"Jen, if you're looking for ways to discredit her you wouldn't have to look far. She's a very clever lady, but not the most credible person in the world. Anyway, it was no secret that she inherited a large sum of money from a distant relative and started up Yellowstone Development Consultancy, taking Alex and the Reverend with her."

"Alex and ... the Reverend?"

"Alex Davis and Kieron Dixon. We called him the Reverend because he could turn a simple presentation into a Biblical epic. They're two of the scruffiest creatures in the world. They'd look more at home in a rock band, but they're both brilliant when it comes to volcanology … Could do with them both here, but Peg got in first."

"But you just said that you could use them both, so why don't you? I mean, you pay more than her … right?"

Fergus sighed; it was perfectly clear to him.

"Look … Kieron likes working with Alex and Alex has always had a bit of a thing for Peg. I mean, don't get me wrong, she's not bad for a woman of her age, but that's just it: she's twenty years older than us. Still, Alex always had a thing for older women. Look, Jen, as fascinating as I find Peg's little outfit, I still don't really understand what you need to know all this for."

"No … Well, that's just it," began Jenny, relishing the chance to be as patronising as Fergus, if only briefly, "You don't need to know."

"Oh, is that right? Okay then, I'll get back to work if that's all right. As there's obviously nothing else you need."

"Okay, okay, Fergus … but this goes no further. The White House has received several letters from Yellowstone Development Consultancy, stating that an eruption at Yellowstone is imminent and that a 1000 km radius needs to be evacuated immediately, if not yesterday. I need to know whether you've picked up anything to confirm this."

"I see, and the rest is checking out their credibility. Right?"

"Right."

"Well, okay, I would find it unlikely that Peg wasn't monitoring Yellowstone. We didn't call her 'Doomsday Peg' for nothing; she's somewhat unhealthily preoccupied with extinction-level volcanoes. And for the record, I would also imagine her equipment is as good as ours, but it will always depend on your translation of the data you get. As far as we are concerned ... No. The area around that caldera is constantly active in one way or another. One geyser dries up, another one starts. Two weeks' increased activity, two weeks' decreased activity. There is nothing to say it's imminent or not imminent, and in real terms you may never get enough warning for a proper evacuation. There isn't any guarantee that it'll ever go up. It could just rumble along until the sun dies, who knows? Don't worry about it. I'll let you know if I think we're in danger."

"Thanks, Fergus. You've been a great help."

"You're welcome, and just so you know, I'll be the first one out of here if it gets dangerous."

"Yeah, thanks again and … well … Bye."

"Yeah, Bye, Jen." She couldn't wait to put the phone down. Fergus was as she always remembered him: reassuringly irritating.

Jenny sank back in her chair and reminded herself of pleasant times they had spent together and was only prevented from embarking on her own trip down memory lane by Charlotte's voice on the intercom:

"It's the President on the line, Ma'am."

"Thank you, Charlotte. Put him through."

Once again saved by the bell, she thought to herself. First the worry of the eruption at Yellowstone and then Fergus. Perhaps the day might settle down after lunch.

"Any news, Jen?"

"Yes, I've just come off the phone to Yellowstone, and 'Our People' assure me that everything is pretty normal down there. They have no reason to expect that an eruption is imminent". This, she figured, should put his mind at rest; there was no real need to give him the full conversation in all its arrogant glory.

"Okay, that's good." He paused for a moment then added, "I think I'll send them a reply this time. Hopefully, that will put an end to their correspondence. What d'you think?"

"I think under the circumstances it's a very good idea, and hopefully you're right—it'll be an end to the matter."

"Thanks, Jen. You've been a great help."

"No trouble, Mr President. Goodbye."

She'd never known Fergus to be wrong about anything, or at least nothing he would ever admit to.

This time.

More than ever before.

He had to be right.

CHAPTER 3

For Peggy Scott, the following day started much the same as any other: by oversleeping. This was followed by a lot of stumbling about and a quick game of 'hunt the car keys' punctuated with various expletives, before finally getting to work where Kieron and Alex were already waiting.

"Need a new alarm clock, Peg?" Alex laughed, nudging her.

"And a new mirror?" Kieron added. She threw him a puzzled look. He nodded towards her jumper,

"Backwards and inside out … hmmm … it'll never catch on."

"Oh, Tee hee!"

They followed her into the lab, still laughing like a couple of school kids, while she made the necessary adjustments to her clothing.

Their lab was a bare-bones unit but, while the surroundings were nowhere near as plush as Yellowstone Geological Centre, the equipment was, as Fergus predicted, every bit as good. She sat down to check the overnight readings, while Kieron, still giggling, picked up the mail and flicked through it.

"Hey, one of these letters is ..." but he was stopped mid-sentence by Peggy, almost blue with shock.

"Oh, shit! ... No! The caldera has risen a few metres overnight, and everything's stopped ... there's nothing: just ... nothing." Her voice tailed away.

"... from the President," he finished. No one commented as they all stared at the readings. Kieron could feel the colour draining from his face and glanced across at Alex, to see the same blank look of horror reflected back at him. The silence, although only minutes, seemed to last for ever; then finally it was broken:

"D'you think the lava heads know?" Alex mumbled shakily.

"S'pose so. It doesn't much matter now." Peg's answer was hauntingly quiet.

"Look, I'm sorry guys, but I'm outta here. If ... If I'm wrong, well ... we'll call it a holiday. You coming Alex?"

Alex looked at Peg.

"You guys go ... Just make sure ... well, make sure people know. Y'know, don't let them think ... no-one tried ... or cared." Kieron nodded.

"I'll make sure you're in the history books." He smiled somewhat weakly at her.

"C'mon Alex, we gotta go."

Alex shook his head.

"I'm staying."

"You're shittin' me, right? For fuck's sake, Alex, c'mon."

"I'm staying ... Now get outta here!" Kieron didn't need telling twice; he was gone. He didn't say goodbye because he neither wanted to hang around nor make it more dramatic than it already was.

"You should'a gone, Alex."

"Where? Where should I go? Where's Kieron gonna fuckin' go?! Where Peg?"

"I don't know. Maybe he'll ... "

"No, he won't; you and I both know that, and ... well ... Kieron knows that too."

"Yeah, I know. And thanks ... for staying, anyway." They smiled at each other and managed a very weak laugh. Realistically, there *was nowhere* to go. More readings were coming in, showing a microquake had started. Alex looked at the reading, turned to Peggy, and with a last feeble attempt at optimism muttered:

"*Maybe* it's okay now."
She glared furiously, while, in a 'weak schoolboy-in-trouble' voice, he added,

"S'not new is it? I mean, well ... we have 'em ... microquakes all the time ... "

"Open the letter." Anything to stop Alex mumbling rubbish.

"What?"

"The letter: the one Kieron said was from the President; we might as well see what he's gotta say."

He obeyed but was shaking so much that actually opening the letter was taking much longer than she'd anticipated.

"Well, what's 'e gotta say then?"

"Dunno yet."

"Aw c'mon, Alex. Give it here."

As he handed her the letter, the first sound was heard coming from Yellowstone. It was deafening, as if every thunderstorm from the last decade had culminated in one place: under the ground at Yellowstone. The agonising roar of a volcano waking after 640,000 years of sleep.

The earthquake that almost immediately accompanied the thundering sound was equally devastating. Within minutes, the ground had taken new form. Peggy and Alex helplessly watched as coffee cups, desk-tidies, and other sundries were hurled around them. The walls shook, doors blew open, and eventually the equipment she had spent so much time using had become nothing more than a memory.

They clung to each other, unaware of the pandemonium outside, partly because they couldn't hear it, but largely because of their own self-consuming terror. Completely unaware of time, they stayed there. Huddled together. Unable to move or speak.

Their unit was based in Cody, about 60 miles from the caldera rim, yet within minutes of the first cataclysmic sound, cracks in the earth's crust began appearing. The fissures along which the magma travelled formed a giant web around the caldera, reaching distances up to 100 miles away, with Peggy and Alex caught in the middle. Both of them were killed by the heat long before the flowing river of hot lava swallowed their charred remains forever.

In the last moments, Alex watched a large part of his life flash before his eyes (only the important stuff though): first girlfriend, first beer, first car, and the time he and Kieron went skinny-dipping at a party in Thailand, only to discover all the girls were transvestites.

Peggy's thoughts were somewhat more profound. She died still wondering why Fergus hadn't seen this coming. How many could have been saved if he had? Her very last thought being, 'Damn you Fergus!!'

The truth is, Fergus *hadn't* seen it coming. Why would he? It hadn't followed any of the normal patterns expected before a major eruption and, for that matter, it still wasn't. There were no large pre-event earthquakes, just a few more of the usual microquakes. The caldera hadn't shown any signs of abnormal swelling until a couple of hours ago. Everything that was happening in hours, would normally take weeks, if not months. Peggy had only seen it because she wanted to. She had wanted to believe every little change was the beginning of a mega-colossal eruption and, despite her attempts to get the area evacuated, she herself would never have left. Volcanoes had been her life and this one, in all its destructive glory, was most definitely her nemesis. The first Fergus had known about it was a phone call, waking him up at 6.30 am, from the night staff at Yellowstone Geological Centre:

"Fergus, it's Yellowstone. We've gotta problem: the caldera's risen a metre in the last hour and all activity has stopped, no fumaroles ... nothing."

"Mmm, it's probably nothing. It did it before, a few years ago. Does anyone else know?"

"Just the staff here ... Oh, yeah, and probably Peg at Yellowstone Development."

"Mm, yeah ... Doomsday Peg ... God help us ... It's bound to be a major catastrophe then." He laughed at the image he had of Peggy waving an 'End of the World is Nigh' placard.

"Look, if anyone's really worried, then ...well ... tell them to go home and take their families on holiday. But keep it low key, eh? Don't want to cause unnecessary panic. I'll get hold of the White House and we'll take it from there. Okay?"

"Yeah, sure ... D'ya think they'll they evacuate?"

"Probably not. There's not enough to go on, really. Like I said, it's done it before. That caldera needs to be a lot higher yet for them to take any real notice. Just take a few days off if you're worried, okay? I'll be down soon anyway, so I'll take a look then."

"See ya later then, Fergus."

"Yeah. Bye."

Deep down, both men knew they wouldn't see each other later. The phone clicked as he placed the handset back on the receiver, and he relayed the message about taking a holiday to all at Yellowstone, which they all rapidly interpreted to mean, 'Get the hell out!'

Fergus had lied: it hadn't done it before, but he knew there was nowhere near enough evidence to convince the White House to organise a full evacuation nor, by the sound of it, really enough time. Racked with guilt, but determined to do something, he stared blankly at the computer screen in his study, struggling for the right words to put in an email to Secretary of State, Jenny Peters. She deserved an apology; she had come to him for help, and he had let her down. Not only her, either: the American people. Somebody as intelligent and self-confident as Fergus needs to find the right words; especially if it is their *last* words.

Eventually he clicked 'send', just as the first sign of activity from Yellowstone was heard: the apocalyptic thundering. Still sat at his desk, gazing aimlessly at nothing, he shared Peggy's last thoughts: Why had he not seen this? How many people could have been saved?

As the first tremors reached his house, he reached into the desk drawer, took out the small handgun he'd kept in case of intruders, and placed the barrel in his mouth. As the complexity of his emotions combined with sheer terror, he took the luxury of closing his eyes and pulling the trigger.

Kieron, too, had only gone a few miles when the first sound of Yellowstone thundering through Wyoming caused the heady mixture of shock and panic to completely overwhelm him. His car started to swerve and the more he tried to gain control of it, the more it swerved. Suddenly it stopped. Kieron took a moment to assess the situation, taking note of the fact that the car *had* actually stopped, and that he was, in fact, still alive. Breathing a sigh of relief, he tried to compose himself enough to get the car going again. It wasn't long before it dawned on him that the car had only stopped because it had crashed into the wall of a motel on route 14. The hood was crumpled, and steam was coming out of the radiator. A brief assessment of the situation drew him to the only conclusion possible: the car was going nowhere. The full hopelessness of the situation became apparent with the realisation that he could feel a crippling, burning sensation coming from his right leg. Reaching down, he felt the splintered bone poking out through the torn skin, and a warm, viscous liquid that he quickly identified as his blood. He was going nowhere. He was trapped in his car, and the ground that was now trembling would soon become the biggest earthquake humankind had ever known. Realising the futility of trying to go anywhere, he scrabbled around in the glove compartment.

"Aah, gotcha!"

A packet of cigarettes and a Reese's 'Fast Break' bar. He had come to the conclusion that all condemned men were entitled to a last meal and cigarette. Taking puffs on the cigarette, whilst simultaneously chewing mouthfuls of chocolate, he briefly amused himself with the idea of Jesus breaking up a Hershey's bar and handing round a pack of cigarettes at the Last Supper, as he watched the buildings progress from a slow shiver to a violent, uncontrollable shaking. He knew that being crushed to death under falling rubble would be the most likely cause of his death. The very last thoughts that Kieron Dixon ever had, as he sat in his car, were probably more due to heavy blood loss than any actual thought. Drifting in and out of consciousness and hallucinating every step of the way, it is very likely that he may well have already died before he was buried forever under falling debris.

The initial sound caused just about everybody in earshot to panic, with most people believing they were under attack from terrorists. Largely because they were unaware of what was to follow, they naively believed their bunkers or basements would protect them but, in reality, those in the epicentre would all be buried alive. However, there were plenty of people who, right up until the ground started to wrench itself apart beneath them, had thought they would survive. They'd expected nothing more than a small microquake, assuming that had it been *really* dangerous then surely the government would have evacuated them.

As the earth ripped apart, hell itself broke loose with vast numbers of its damned inhabitants rushing around outside screaming, as if making as much noise as possible would save them. Others just huddled in corners, paralysed by fear. Mothers clung to their children, praying for a miracle; a few even smothered their babies, believing that to be a less horrific death. Husbands shot their wives, children, and even the family pets before turning the gun on themselves, taking the faster, less painful route to the same inevitable outcome. Death.

As the caldera dragged itself along the newly formed fissures, it continued to rise and swell. The noise grew louder as new ridges grew into cliffs around the old caldera rim. The force of the earthquake which by now was completely off the Richter scale, had caused tsunamis in Yellowstone Lake. West Thumb and Grant village, once picturesque visitor centres, were little more than a muddy swamp littered with the splintered remains of the buildings. The sounds of picnicking families, playing children, and laughter would soon be replaced by the angry roar of the super-volcano and the waves now crashing on the shore.

Still in the firm grip of the mega-quake, the next phase of the waking super-volcano occurred. The thunderous noise, which had continued relentlessly since the beginning, was now being enhanced by a series of rock-shattering explosions. These were accompanied by a column of ash, sulphur dioxide, lava, mud, and rocks combined with a cocktail of lethal gases that reached majestically into the atmosphere. Pyroclastic flows made up of the same poisonous ingredients charged across the land at several hundred miles an hour, indiscriminately incinerating everything within a thousand-mile radius.

The Government's planned evacuation, which would only have been implemented on 'their peoples" command, of a 200-mile radius would have been utterly futile. People on the outskirts had more time to escape, although there were the usual 'prefer to die in my own home' who just didn't bother, and a few who just didn't believe it would travel that far, making the death toll somewhat higher than was actually necessary.

As the earthquake continued, a growing fissure spread out from Jackson at the southern entrance of Yellowstone National Park and headed south-west through Utah, followed rapidly by the unstoppable pyroclastic inferno. It's devastating journey took it straight to Los Angeles, at the heart of the San Andreas Fault.

The world-splitting quake had left a rift in the ground that made the Grand Canyon look like a ditch (although that was unlikely to look the same now). Mercilessly it continued its path of destruction, heading along the San Andreas Fault, where it shook the entire coastline. It left a metre-wide trench from Alaska to Argentina, with San Quentin, La Paz, and Panama City being virtually destroyed in the process.

The Malibu beach houses, once the coveted holiday homes of the rich and famous, sank into the liquefied sand as it became one with the ocean. Homes and possessions were swept away, until nothing remained of the glitz and glamour lifestyle once present there.

The quake triggered a series of smaller volcanic eruptions throughout California, and only divine intervention somehow prevented the long valley caldera from being amongst them.

The Diablo canyon and San Onofre nuclear power-plants automatically shut down with the first hint of a tremor and, although they were probably the strongest buildings in California, they too collapsed like a house of cards. A lethal combination of the power-plants collapsing, volcanic and seismic activity, and the fires raging along the coast, meant that radioactive materials were leaked into the environment. The questions with no answer as yet, were how much? And what?

The sheer force of the quake had destroyed the western coast, rocked the ocean bed, generating a series of tsunamis that sped across the Pacific one after another. The waves, which varied from 200 miles to 900 miles in width, travelled at speeds of up to 600 miles per hour, relentlessly battering the coastlines of China, Japan, the Arctic Circle, and parts of Australia. Even after the quake had died down, the aftershocks were enough to keep the killer water coming. The speeding water, which appeared as no more than a large ripple on a stormy day at sea, rapidly approached the shoreline. The ocean receded as if to make way for the guest of honour, which would be the next thing (and possibly the last thing) anyone saw. A wall of water, rising up to a height of 50 miles or more, before it crashed onto the shore destroying everything in its path.

Fiji, Hawaii, and the Solomon Islands (plus other small Pacific Islands) were so battered by the relentless onslaught that very few people, if any, survived. Trees were uprooted and buildings levelled, while people and possessions alike were simply washed away forever.

The first sign of life had been heard from Yellowstone at around 9am, and by midday the landscape had completely changed and the world everyone knew was lost forever. Torrential rainstorms had joined the unstoppable chaos and volcanic ash, now damp and heavy, was being blown by a south-easterly wind across America as far as the Gulf of Mexico. Travel by air was impossible and any planes already en route had to make emergency landings. Ships were redirected to the nearest ports. Travel by road in the States had become so chaotic that there was gridlock on most routes. Terrified people were left with no option but to seek shelter, where possible, on foot, as the human instinct to survive fought against the sheer hopelessness of their situation.

CHAPTER 4

The first knowledge of the eruption reached Gerry McQuillan at the same time it reached everyone else in America: with the loud thunderous sound that signified Yellowstone was awake. His immediate thought was that it must be a terrorist explosion somewhere downtown, and he switched the television on for confirmation.

What he saw was the last thing he expected. A couple of die- hard reporters from Cody, obviously not realising the gravity of the situation, had tried filming the incident. The panic and fear on the face of any individual as they realise death is imminent is normally a very private thing, but for a few brief moments these inhabitants of Cody shared it with an entire nation.

An instant feeling of guilt and nausea hit Gerry McQuillan straight in the stomach.

"Dear God, what have I done?" he sighed, holding his head in his hands. "What have I done?"

He needed to talk to Jenny. She was the only one who would realise. She knew he had had an option; she knew he could have saved them. She too had heard the volcano, and like Gerry believed it to be the work of terrorists; she was about to switch on the television when the intercom buzzed.

"Ma'am, the President's on line one."

"Thanks, Charlotte. Put him through."

"Can you come to my office please? I need to speak with you in private if that's okay?"

"Yeah, sure. I'll be right there."

"Thank you." Before she could say anything else, the phone clicked dead.

"Charlotte, I'll be in a meeting; if anyone wants me, well … they'll just have to wait."

"Okay. Message received and understood." she joked. "But before you go Ma'am, there's an email for you. From that Fergus at Yellowstone. I don't suppose it's anything personal as it came through on this address, but … well, I'd like you to take a look anyway."

Charlotte looked so confused by it all that she felt compelled to take a look. It simply read:

"I'm sorry."

It wasn't even signed, but the email address was enough to know it was from Fergus.

Jenny was now completely confused. Firstly, in all the years she'd known Fergus she had never known him to apologise for anything, even when he was solely in the wrong. Secondly, what was he apologising for?

"I'd better get going or I'll be late. You were right to mention it. Thanks."

"Okay. See you later, Ma'am."

On the way to the President's office, she tried to figure out the strange apologetic email, but was still none the wiser by the time she knocked on the door.

"Come in."

"Morning, Mr. President," she said, closing the door.

"Sit down, Jen. I need you to see this." He sounded concerned, more so than she had ever seen before. They had been through many crises over the years, but this was something different. This was a whole new level of concern.

"What is it, Gerry? Is it terrorists? What have they done?"

The lack of colour in his face made her equally as anxious as he appeared—obviously something was very wrong. He nodded towards the television; she stared at the screen, not really taking it all in. A mixture of disbelief and horror swept over her as reports of more and more devastation just kept coming. She watched the repeat of the Cody reports and the more she saw, the more sense the email from Fergus made.

"I've scheduled an emergency meeting of the National Security Council for 11am. Maybe by then we will have an idea of what exactly is going on down there, what else to expect, and hopefully be able to work out a rescue and aid strategy."

"Er ... mm ... yes ... of course," she replied, still reeling from the images of Cody.

"I could have changed this, couldn't I? ... Jen?" His voice trailed to a whisper. She didn't answer instantly because there was no right answer.

"You made the only decision you could under the circumstances. You asked the right people and got the wrong answer; it's not your fault, Gerry. Those people ... the ones, you know, who kept writing ... well, I don't really think they knew, not really. Not that it would be, well ... well, like this."

"Oh, God Jen, what must they have thought when they read that letter? They deserved better."

"I dunno, but there's nothing you can do to change it right now. However, maybe the meeting will throw some light on the situation."

"Yeah, you're right ... as always." She smiled as she left to prepare for the meeting.

Back in her office, the phone hadn't stopped ringing. Charlotte had put the television on and, by the look on her face, was obviously trying to get to grips with the situation.

"That Fergus you spoke to, yesterday …"

"What? Has he rung?"

"Erm … no," she continued, a little confused by Jenny's sudden interruption.

"I was only going to say it's frightening to think you talk to a person one day and they're … you know … gone the next."

"What? Oh … mm … yes. I suppose it is."

Charlotte wasn't being insensitive; she simply wasn't aware of Jenny's relationship with Fergus. Up until then, it hadn't really occurred to Jenny that Fergus might be dead. Replaying over and over in her head was the last conversation she had with him. He had sounded so confident this wouldn't happen that it seemed highly unlikely he would have escaped.

By the start of the meeting, as much data had been collected as humanly possible. There were no other television broadcasts from nearby, as no one could get close enough to actually achieve anything; they could offer nothing more than speculation. The best information came from satellite imaging and geologists. The caldera at Yellowstone had been a volcanic time bomb for centuries, and there was hardly a geologist left in the world who didn't have some interest in it. Because of the attention it drew, there had been several different groups with seismometers, tiltmeters, and global positioning systems strategically located around the caldera. This was now helpful in confirming what exactly was happening.

Now everyone present knew not only what had taken place earlier, but also with the pyroclastic surges coming from the volcano and the earthquake ripping through the country, that it obviously wasn't over yet.

Several field geologists had been brought in to provide their predictions on how long it would continue, and what else could be expected. In between the somewhat over-enthusiastic talks from the 'experts', which focussed on looming tidal waves and the possibility of triggering other volcanic hotspots, there were also a fair number of very morbidly inventive but nonetheless accurate predictions, including the earthquake reaching the San Andreas Fault, volcanic winters, and the possible extinction of mankind; not to mention looting, rioting, and a whole host of opportunities for terrorism.

In view of all this, the President took the only real course of action available.

"This was not an easy decision to make, but I feel I have no other choice than to declare a federal state of emergency. You know what to do, so I trust you'll set the ball rolling." He directed the last part of his sentence to the Secretary of Homeland Security, who nodded in acknowledgement.

The ball rolled like this: the President decides on the course of action to be taken, in this instance a federal state of emergency, he passes it to the Secretary of Homeland Security who in turn passes it to the State Emergency Co-ordination Team (S.E.C.T.).

S.E.C.T. had originally been the Federal Emergency Management Agency but, due to growing fears about 'shadow governments' either waiting to take over the government, secretly running the government, or other such nonsense stirred up by conspiracy theorists, the name had been 'downgraded' to make them sound less threatening. Their role (which had remained exactly the same) was to try and reduce the impact or severity of any hazard and ensure there were the resources and manpower to deal with the hazard. Once they had done that, immediate action would be taken primarily to save life and, if possible, preserve the environment, homes, and of course the economy. When they had the aforementioned hazard under control, then they could set about rebuilding the community, restoring services, power, and eventually homes and jobs, etc. In this instance, they certainly had their work cut out for them, and all they would really be able to do would be to pick up the pieces of a broken country. They couldn't reduce the severity of it, they didn't have anywhere near the resources to cope with it, and there was no way of getting close enough to save anyone.

Having set that particular ball rolling, President McQuillan turned his attention to the rest of his administration.

"Due to the high probability of looting and rioting that tends to accompany these situations, I feel it may be necessary to impose a state of martial law. Just for the moment, unless anybody has any objections or alternative suggestions."

There were no suggestions or any real objections. The meeting continued for a couple of hours with health issues and public information being high on the agenda. The problem was that throughout the meeting, the crisis was still continuing. As soon as an agreement was reached on dealing with one issue, something else happened. This made it very difficult to come up with an overall strategy.

Television stations and journalists around the remainder of the country had spent the entire day trying for pictures, stories, and, of course, comments from the President. Several of them were firmly rooted outside the White House. It wasn't until lunchtime, with the country still firmly in the grip of the worst geological event in recorded history, that they finally got what they had been waiting for. The President gave a speech to what was left of the nation:

"Good afternoon. Today, it is with great sorrow that I must inform you that America is, as of now, in a federal state of emergency.

At around 9 o'clock this morning, the caldera at Yellowstone National Park erupted, triggering a series of cataclysmic earthquakes. These earthquakes are still ongoing, with the full extent of the damage and tragic loss of human life not yet known.

Due to the eruption, volcanic ash has entered the atmosphere and is currently being blown across the United States. This ash should not be inhaled as it is likely to contain harmful toxins; as a result of this you are strongly advised to remain in your homes. Paramilitary troops will be issuing anti-smog masks to all areas that are still accessible. Communication with these troops should be brief, stating only the number of masks required. Do not ask for more than your household needs: one mask per person. In apartment blocks it is recommended that a spokesperson be nominated, to save time.

Do not leave your homes to check on relatives and friends.

Please do not telephone the emergency services, as the lines need to be kept clear.

Emergency aid ***will*** be distributed, as soon as is physically possible.

Because of the severity of the situation, we are aware of the possibility of looting and rioting. This would only add to an already hazardous situation, therefore martial law has been imposed for the time being. This is only intended as a temporary measure, to maintain order and to enable aid and rescue teams to do their job unhindered.

It is the responsibility of each and every American citizen to ensure that this crisis passes as smoothly as is possible.
This is indeed a tragedy for America, but we are a strong nation and by working

together we can survive. That is, after all, what makes America great.

"Thank you for listening."

It wasn't only America: pretty much the entire world was in crisis and communication between world leaders continued long into the night, consisting largely of speculation on global effects and how best to deal with the long-term repercussions. The world, it seemed, was shocked into uniting forces. Political arguments and cultural differences had no place in the world. Not today.

Much of the world, and those Americans who still had power, spent most of their time glued to a television somewhere, watching the live reports that switched to different networks as power failures continued to spread out from the epicentre. Any live reports continued to be punctuated by re-runs of the Cody reporters in the first few moments of Yellowstone and their last few moments of life.

The broadcast began with a very nervous young reporter stood on Southfork Road. Nobody would ever know why he and the cameraman were there; the best guess would be that they were on their way to another incident when the volcano started, and they just decided to take advantage of a 'once in a lifetime scoop'.

With his microphone turned up to filter out any background noise and taking a deep breath, he blurted out something that may have been speculation about Yellowstone and noise, but even with the filters turned up there was no chance of being heard above the volcano. The only bit anybody really heard was his name, probably because that was the only thing he knew for certain. Nobody saw him die; they heard him and the cameraman shouting, then they saw the camera shake followed by horrible eerie silence.

By nightfall, the earthquake had slowed to a barely noticeable tremor, and the tsunamis had finally subsided. The smaller Californian volcanoes had calmed, with only Mount Shasta remaining active: a 15000 ft high stratovolcano formidable in its own right, but fortunately not erupting with any great force. Yellowstone, however, was continuing its magnificent reign of destruction and, as yet showed no signs of slowing down. With its plume stretching far up into the atmosphere, and pyroclastic surges flowing across the country, Yellowstone had rendered America helpless. It would remain that way until the volcano fell back into another 640,000-year sleep.

All the White House staff and emergency services were able to do was pump themselves full of Orexin and coffee and settle in for a long night.

CHAPTER 5

The following day a smoky twilight haze covered most of the American continent, with the Western United States and parts of Canada seeing no sunrise and no daylight. The hot lava flow from the unrelenting super-volcano was the only light shining in the morning sky. Yellowstone would continue its reign of terror until late on Hallowe'en, with the same agonising roar that had heralded its awakening echoing around the United States.

On the seventh day there was silence, and with that silence came hope. Unfortunately, this hope was to be quickly forgotten when, a week later, the global death toll from the eruption was announced: approximately 200,000,000 people lost their lives that week, 70,000,000 of whom were Americans.

This figure was just the beginning. Torrential rainstorms had added mudslides and floods to the already impossible rescue operation. Men, women, and children, desperately clambered for safety, only to get swept along by the overwhelming force of the liquefied mud. Almost the entire USA was buried under half a metre of volcanic ash, with the vast majority of wooden houses caving in under the weight. There was nowhere across the entire American continent that hadn't been affected by the Yellowstone volcano. It seemed there was no end to the damage it could inflict on an unsuspecting world.

Rescue workers fought their way through ash and rubble hoping to find survivors, but sadly they were few and far between. There were a couple of miracles: heart-warming stories where people who had been trapped under thick ash and debris had somehow managed to stay alive. A few people had been forced to self-amputate trapped limbs in an attempt to free themselves. Most of these however had died later, either as a result of heavy blood-loss or septicaemia.

Families who lay huddled together littered the towns and countryside alike, their charcoal bodies reminiscent of the last days of Pompeii. Fire-fighters worked round the clock against the blazing towns and cities, where fires were rapidly spreading out of control. Despite their brave attempts, it was a futile exercise with most fires eventually being left to simply burn themselves out.

The footage of families who had abandoned their cars and were traipsing across the ash-covered remains of America was shown repeatedly throughout the world: the soon to be familiar scene of hungry, exhausted mothers, numb with the cold, dragging small children through the forests of corpses.

Multitudes of people who, only a few hours ago, lived on high salaries in comfortable homes were now cold, wet, and on the verge of collapse, desperately searching for aid and shelter. Apparently these were the *lucky* ones.

Even death was no longer the final indignity, with corpses being scavenged for food, clothing, weapons, or any other serviceable items. Of course, anybody who was near death or looked like they might soon be near death, could conveniently become a corpse. One popular headline featured an old man who had self-amputated his left arm after it had become trapped, only to later be shot and scavenged by looters. It was never entirely clear what useful commodity they had actually gained from this wretched individual.

President McQuillan held the expected press conference to offer the usual condolences, and of course to ask for voluntary help from retired nurses, doctors, and just about anybody who could help 'rebuild America'. Other world leaders also came forward to offer their condolences, although offering aid wasn't possible due to all shipping lanes being closed and air travel restrictions.

The shipping lane closures were mainly due to the possibility of radioactive pollution from the destruction of the Californian nuclear power plants. Air travel restrictions were brought into force largely because of the current weather conditions. Although the rainstorms had gradually become less torrential, the rain had mixed with sulphur particles from the eruption to form a new hazard: acid rain. This, at the very least, would mean poor visibility and therefore an increased risk of accidents. Realistically, there couldn't have been many people who wanted to go on holiday as most holiday destinations would be more hazardous than the flight.

These closures had been agreed by world leaders as temporary safety measures, pending an emergency U.N. conference that had been scheduled for a week later. This would not only give the White House a chance to assess the extent of the damage America had sustained but would also allow them time to ascertain any potential risks to other areas from various eruption-related problems. Likewise, China and its neighbouring countries, all of which had suffered excessive damage to their coastal areas from the tsunamis, also had a chance to compile their damage reports.

This conference, like most U.N. conferences, was held over the internet on a secure quantum encryption coded ISP.

Special internet conference rooms had become features in all leadership residences. Large rooms with monitors built into the walls along with web cams and translators. These meant that conferences could still take place, but without the need to travel, which at this moment in time was an absolute Godsend.

President McQuillan and his secretary of state, Jenny Peters, took their places in the conference room for one of the most solemn U.N. meetings in history.

The following items were on the agenda for discussion: the loss of several islands in the pacific, whose inhabitants had just been 'washed away'; the uninhabitable state of Japan, whose coastlines had been severely battered, causing collapsed buildings, loss of power throughout, and of course the countless loss of human lives; and the inevitable economic repercussions. America's economy had almost entirely collapsed, with stock-markets crashing world-wide. China, Malaysia, Vietnam, and Indonesia had all suffered economic blows as well as power failure and extensive human loss.

The first agenda item was their greatest concern: the impending volcanic winter, which required immediate emergency measures to ensure there was enough food and heating for the coming months. At the end of the day, the agreement of cease-fires and temporary peace treaties were paramount for the duration of the crisis.

A workforce, medical supplies, and food were supplied by those countries who could afford it. The biggest surprise was the first ever donation, of any kind, by The Vatican. However, if they had known how long the crisis would continue, or how short their own food supplies would become over the next two years, it is highly unlikely that any of them would have been quite so willing to help.

A week later, shipping lanes were re-opened. A spokesperson for the White House stated that while 'it appeared **some** radioactive waste **might** have leaked into the sea and localised areas around the power plants, there was **absolutely no evidence** to suggest that levels were high enough to pose any threat to mankind.' Of course, just to make sure the public was in no doubt as to how safe they were, the statement was punctuated by a lot of references to **x-rays**, **low-level waste**, and the **becquerels** that measure radioactive contamination. This was designed to reinforce the population's belief that they were **in no possible danger**.

The reality of the situation meant the need to import food and fuel outweighed the contamination risks. It was a definite death as opposed to a probable death, helped by a blissfully ignorant population and a government that was keeping its political fingers crossed. Just on the off chance that it should all go horribly wrong, there was the usual 'head in the sand whilst lying through the back teeth' contingency plan.

Flight was only permitted in emergencies: rescue, aid, and, of course, any other activity the military deemed an emergency. All commercial flights were cancelled until further notice.

The questions of nuclear weapon caches, military bases, factories, and other potential toxin storage within the 'eruption zone' were later raised by an extremely concerned public.

Obviously, the White House vehemently denied the existence of any military facilities in that area containing nuclear, chemical, or any other stockpiles of weapons of mass destruction.

It was ironic that the American government was under the same scrutiny from its own citizens that it had put the

Middle East under, over a decade ago. As the saying goes: 'What goes around comes around.'

The American people didn't totally believe the White House any more than the White House had believed the Middle East several years earlier, but fortunately for Gerry McQuillan the people of America weren't in a position to start any wars. Apart from anything else, most of them had lost someone in the Yellowstone tragedy, so for the moment they wanted to believe him.

Over the coming months the temperature gradually dropped, finally levelling out eight degrees Celsius lower than normally expected. This was a global phenomenon, causing severe crop failure, with freak weather conditions being recorded world-wide.

In already cold climates, ice storms brought power failures, and food shortages as travel became virtually impossible; black ice, blocked roads, and frozen diesel were the most common problems. Soup-kitchens were opened to feed the hungry, but they gradually diminished in number as supplies became increasingly harder to come by.

Along with the food and power shortages came increased risk from hypothermia, influenza, pneumonia, and frostbite. Hospitals became unable to supply the necessary medical attention in areas where supplies couldn't get through to them.

Crime went hand in hand with the food crisis; looting was on the increase in most cities and towns, and it seemed that if the cold didn't kill people, looters or the lack of food probably would.

Even in warmer climates, it was a lot colder than normal with insufficient resources in most areas to cope with the temperature drop and unusual weather patterns.

Farmers were forced into slaughtering livestock to try and meet the food demands. More meat was consumed over the next couple of years, cholesterol being very low on the list of health concerns, and vegetarians were forced to seriously reconsider their dietary habits. The internet and television were full of information about preserving meat by salting in areas with restricted or no power. This did not take into account the fact that people with no power can neither watch television nor use the internet.

Between 2045 and 2047, the number of deaths globally was estimated to be around two billion, entirely due to starvation, cold related illnesses, radiation sickness, or poor sanitation. There was also the human factor, which included suicides, addiction-related deaths, (accidental drug overdoses, alcohol poisoning etc.), murders, or injuries resulting in death.

The media had turned their attention to how people survived in the very remote parts of the world, filling their pages with stories of murder and cannibalism. None of this could be proved of course, but the public lapped it up.

Another wave of illness was beginning to emerge, with radiation sickness claiming its first few victims. Initially these were fairly localised to the power plants and could be classified on government documents as 'an acceptable number of deaths within the estimated pollution zone'. Over time, as these spread out, covering a larger area and the death toll rose, it became evident that this was no longer just a national, but a global, problem.

More media-hype followed, with conspiracy claims that it was not only the power plants that were to blame, but also weapons stockpiles. This fuelled stories about deliberate government cover-ups and speculation as to what had really been kept in 'Area 51'.

The truth was far more simplistic than that: the White House had permitted potentially contaminated food to be distributed. More accurately, the food shortages had made the decision for them, with logic dictating that *any* food was better than *none*.

People in towns and cities had the highest chance of survival, but they also had a new plague to contend with: 'Religious Mania'. Newspapers had their 'situations vacant' columns replaced by 'Repent the Lord is upon you', 'Follow Christ and be saved', 'Armageddon Cometh', and of course the ever familiar, 'The End of the World Is Nigh'. Obviously, salvation and eternal life was available to all, for a designated fee that would usually be cash, food, or fuel. Due to the economic problems, God no longer accepted all major credit cards.

The other side, of course, added their ten cents' worth with 'Your God has Abandoned You', 'Lucifer Is among Us', 'Where Is Your God Now', and so on. Most people had acquired a new religious view perspective – having 'seen the light', with 'practising agnostics' only really existing among scientists and the ruling classes.

After all was said and done, the Christian fanatics had plenty to argue their point with: devastating earthquakes, worse than the world had ever seen before; the sun was blackened by volcanic ash; there were burning lakes of sulphur; the moon didn't turn blood red, but a few darkened sunsets could be made to fit the bill if required; death in abundance, with numerous plagues and severe famine; the worst crime-wave ever, with violence and looting running hand in hand. As far as wild beasts were concerned, a starving population was fast becoming the most lethal beast humankind could find on Earth. 'Eternal damnation', 'Fire and Brimstone', 'The Antichrist' (although he didn't have a clear identity), and any other 'made to measure' quote from the Book of Revelation found its way into the classified ads of every available newspaper; in fact, in just about any media source that was available.

The world was still changing, and people's attitudes were changing with it, especially towards each other. In the hungry ghettos, best friends could easily begin to take on the appearance of a favourite meal, but in areas like the White House, friendships became more important. Loyal employees often made trustworthy friends. In this cold harsh reality, friendships were all there was. Subsequently, the White House, like many other State residences, became far less formal than it had ever been before the eruption.

The President and Jenny Peters had always been good friends and now it became so much more important to maintain that friendship. Prior to the eruption Jenny had lived alone, but the rioting, looting, and general state of lawlessness meant that she, along with several other members of White House staff, now resided in the guest apartments. This was a safety measure: anybody choosing to go home obviously could, but if there was no one to go home to why bother? Putting themselves at unnecessary risk was not only foolish, but also very impractical. The White House, like every other State residence immediately affected by Yellowstone, was operating on a skeleton staff. Losing more staff would only cause more problems.

This new White House had other social aspects to it: meetings were much less formal, and Mrs McQuillan now preferred to be called Nina instead of Ma'am and was seen far more often around the White House. Having been unable to have children herself, she adopted this new role of White House matriarch quite willingly.

Gerry McQuillan spent each morning having coffee and reading the papers with Jenny Peters. She would scan through the New York Times whilst he read the Washington Daily Post cover to cover.

"Same old shit ... diff'rent day," remarked Jenny, during one of these coffee sessions.

"Yeah, I know Jen, but we need to know what's going on out there. It's our job ... I mean ... if we don't know what's happening, how will we know what to do about it?"

"I s'pose. But I still don't know how you can be bothered with all those religious nuts though, they're so depressing," she commented, watching him work his way through the classifieds.

"I dunno ... they have some amusement value. Anyway, it's not as miserable as the news."

"I think you need a holiday."

"Yeah, you're probably right. Mmm ... now let me see ... maybe a trip to the mountains ... perhaps. No, I've got it ... A nice villa overlooking the beach ... Malibu's nice this time of year. "

"Yeah, yeah, very funny. But I was actually being serious. Well ... maybe not a holiday, but time out. You've been working real long hours lately with all this ... and ... well ... "

"Well, what? ... What?"

"Well ... "

"Oh, please stop saying 'well' and get to the point."

"Well ..." He rolled his eyes, and she knew she would have to say something other than 'well'.

"Oh, all right. Nina was saying ..."

"Mmm?"

"Look, Gerry, she's worried about your health: something about headaches. She only told me, not anyone else."

"Oh"

"Is that it? ... 'Oh'?"

As she spoke, he caught sight of an advert in the paper. He looked up and placing his hands behind his head, leant back in the chair. He nodded, smacked his lips together slowly, and serenely added,

"You know what? You're right, Jen. I *do* need a holiday or at least ... like you said, time out."

Jen was somewhat confused by the sudden about turn, but equally flattered by the fact that he actually took any notice of her. A very confident, if not somewhat smug, smile lit up her face. She headed for the door, still beaming, although a bit baffled by how easy it had all been.

"Er, Jen ... Can we keep this low key? Don't mention it to anyone ... I don't want loads of concerns about my health."

"Yeah, sure ... I understand."

"Oh, yeah ... Don't say anything about it to Nina either; she'll assume I must be really ill and worry even more."

She nodded in agreement.

She understood why he didn't want the staff to know: in case they deemed him unfit to be President. Nina? ... Well, that made sense too, as she was the worrying type. What she didn't understand, was *why* he had agreed so easily.

However, much she liked to think it was her powers of persuasion over the most influential man in the world, it wasn't, although he was quite happy for her to think that. In reality, it had much more to do with the timing of their conversation.

Once he was alone, he turned his attention to the advert he'd noticed earlier. On the surface it looked no different to any other, but he recognised the difference.

SUFFER THE FIRES OF HELL
FOR ETERNITY
UNLESS YOU
REPENT NOW
For further information and to donate contact:
THE PEOPLE'S LIGHT and UNIFICATION CHURCH
Washington P.O. Box 36993

This was why he read the adverts every day, and this was why he'd so readily agreed to time off. This was Luc, he was sure of it.

Light and Unification Church—L.U.C.—and a P.O. Box divisible by three. That was how it worked; all he had to do was be available for the next 48 hours and Luc would do the rest.

Luc only ever contacted the *Premiers* on his list, never their *vices or deputies*, and even then, only when it became necessary to meet with them. This was always done via an advert in one of their main newspapers.

On the surface it seemed a primitive contact method, but Luc distrusted the internet and telephones. He considered them far too easy to bug, believing that any three-year-old with a games console could probably hack into most computer systems. The classifieds were only read by people who needed to read them: unlike phones and computers, they had no real entertainment value.

This would normally be the newspaper printed in the city of the leadership's residence.

His contact adverts never stood out from the others and could be under any classified section. Somewhere within the advert, three words would be in the same line, whose initial letters would spell Luc. Where conjunctions were present, the acronym would show the L, the U, and the C in capital letters. The only other give-away to show it was Luc would be a P.O. Box number that was easily divisible by three. Of course, occasionally this would occur by chance, in which case the premier in question would end up having a couple of days off for nothing.

Gerry McQuillan hoped this was not one of those false alarms. He wondered how Luc would arrange the meeting; he checked the micro disc he was given when he came to office. The last sentence stated quite clearly, 'Arrange to go to Camp David the morning after my advert, around 8 a.m. I will do the rest. Luc.'

He had a sneaking suspicion that Luc must be ex-Special Forces or similar; this would explain his apparent invisibility. A sort of scientifically minded Rambo character, if such a thing existed.

Nina appeared in the office doorway.

"Hello, just thought I'd pop in on my way to see Jenny."

"Come in, love. I wanted a word anyway."

"Sounds suspicious." She laughed, sat down opposite him, placed her elbows on the table, rested her head in her hands, and gazed affectionately across the table.

"C'mon then, I'm all ears."

"Well, actually, I've decided to take your advice. I'm taking a couple of days off."

"Oooh, that's a first. You taking advice, I mean. So, when's all this happening?"

"Tomorrow morning; I'm heading over to Camp David."

"Great!"

"The only thing is ... I thought I'd go ... well ... alone. If that's okay with you?"

"I s'pose." She tried to not sound too disappointed, but he could tell that she was.

"I just need a few days' solitude; it's been a bit much lately and ... and I promise next time we'll go together. And for longer ... and ..."

"And what?"

"And ... I love you, of course."

She smiled, "Okay. You win."

"Good. That's settled then." She got up, walked around the table, and kissed him, adding, "I'd better go and pack for you then, eh?"

He smiled as he watched her leave the room.

These days, there was a staff meeting every afternoon to keep on top of any new developments. It was at this meeting that the President informed the staff he was taking 48 hours leave.

"So, Ashley will be in charge over the next couple of days, and I don't envisage any problems that cannot be dealt with. I will see you all on Friday. Thank you for your attention."

That last sentence meant do 'not disturb unless it's a code red situation', which with the current peace treaties was extremely unlikely.

With that, the Oval Office was handed over to Vice President Ashley Jefris. He was normally a very ambitious person who would have jumped at the chance of the Presidency, but since the eruption he'd been quite content to take a back seat in things.

With everybody informed, Gerry McQuillan went back to wondering exactly how Luc would do the rest.

CHAPTER 6

Luc was an enigma. Everything about him was densely shrouded in an unsolvable mystery.

There was no record of his birth or any other aspect of his life, no record of any school or college he may have attended, yet clearly he was very well-educated. There were absolutely no traces of any bank details, passport, driver's licence, or a social security number that could be linked to him. Yet those who had met him knew that he did have money, considerable amounts of it in fact and that he not only travelled but did so quite regularly. What they didn't know was *how*, when there was absolutely nothing to show where he came from, where he lived, or even if Luc was really his name.

There was a greater chance of finding either the Holy Grail or Atlantis, than there was of finding one shred of evidence that could prove Luc had ever existed. As it is impossible to contact someone who doesn't exist, the only people who ever met Luc were the ones that he contacted: a select group of world leaders: Presidents, Prime Ministers, Royalty, or similar: whoever, in his view, had the most power within their government.

Luc was very rarely talked about by these leaders for several reasons. The most likely one was that most Premiers are well-practised in the art of secrecy, and fully aware that nothing is ever gained by careless talk. There was also the fact that trying to tell their governments they had been secretly contacted to attend a meeting in an unknown location, by a man who didn't exist *and* who they knew nothing about, would most likely have them rapidly removed from office and safely tucked away in a lunatic asylum.

There must have been the odd occasion when a Premier had been overheard talking about him, as Luc did briefly obtain mythical status among higher-ranking government officials. That was, however, back in the late twentieth century with no real mention of him since then. At the time, theories about his identity had included 'Mafia Godfather', or 'Head of the Illuminati' as favourites. A few less-popular ideas suggested that he was of extra-terrestrial origin. Very occasionally, it had even been suggested that he was an angel, demon, or the second coming of Christ.

Of course, there was no evidence to support any of these theories, so he remained a myth and, as far as Luc was concerned, he preferred it that way.

Anyway, these days the Illuminati had a much more credible notoriety attached to them.

The current chosen few on Luc's list were:

President Gerry McQuillan ... U.S.A.
Prime Minister Ella Jameson ... Great Britain
President Tian Shi Wu ... China
President Felix Nikolaevich Kurakin ... Russia
Prime Minister Steve Cooper ... Australia
Crown Prince Ghazal ... Saudi Arabia
Prime Minister Priyanka Joshi ... India
Prime Minister Eitan Keshner ... Israel
President Arubel Christakis ... Greece
President Akil Naguib ... Egypt
Pope Gregory XVIII ... Vatican City

As far as Gerry was aware, the first contact Luc had with any of these countries had been back in the late 1940s to organise the construction of the infamous Area 51. Since then, meetings took place randomly every few years; the last meeting was shortly before Gerry McQuillan came into office. Consequently, the only time Luc's name had actually been mentioned to him was during a very private conversation with the previous President, just before he was sworn into office.

It was during this conversation that Gerry McQuillan received the microchip that contained information on a top-secret agenda; an agenda that had apparently been in operation for the last sixty years. In amongst all the data contained on the microchip was information on what was *really* hidden in Area 51 and several other similar facilities.

Where each of the listed heads of state concealed their microchip was entirely up to them, as long as it was safe and remained secret. Previous Heads of State never spoke about Luc or mentioned any of the information held on the microchip. Once they left office, it appeared as if they no longer remembered it; whether this was due to a memory-erasing drug, a neurotransmitter, blackmail, or just violent threats, nobody knew. Except Luc. As nobody else in the country knew of Luc, nobody was ever likely to ask any questions. In theory, these Premiers had forgotten something nobody else had been aware they knew in the first place. One thing that was very clear, was that Luc didn't take any chances. Secret meant, just that. Secret!

This would be the first time that President McQuillan had met Luc and while he believed him to be ex-Special Forces or similar, he was also aware that by now he must be a very old man. Nonetheless, it did not make the whole affair any the less intriguing.

Due to the chaos caused by the Yellowstone eruption and its subsequent after-effects, the White House was still operating with a reduced staff. This meant that the motorcade and entourage of security guards that usually accompanied the President just wasn't possible. Instead, all that could be reasonably spared were four security guards, one of whom would have to be the driver. It had been agreed therefore that although it was only a relatively short distance to Camp David it would be much safer to fly, and it could be classified as one of those instances where flight was necessary.

It was 8 o'clock the following morning when President Gerry McQuillan left the White House with four security guards for the short drive to a nearby disused airfield. Two in the front of the car, including the driver, and two in the back (one either side of him), but he didn't feel particularly safe. Even though Washington D.C. had got off lightly compared to other areas of the U.S.A., it still had an abundance of homeless people and a higher than usual crime rate.

As they drove to the small airfield, he felt one of the security guards reach into his coat pocket and an uneasiness crept over him; for the moment he decided to say nothing.

Looking out of the window at the city, he saw the posters announcing the arrival of a biblical Armageddon. He wondered at the senseless destruction. He questioned whether God really existed and, if he did, exactly what sort of god would he have to be to allow this level of destruction, et al. In fact, he was so deeply engrossed in his own religious contemplations that the car slowed to a halt without him even noticing.

"We're here. Mr President," announced one of the security guards, forcing him to become aware of the fact that they'd stopped.

"Sorry, I was miles away ..."

"That's okay, Sir. The plane's waiting."

Once out of the car he was aware of the cold. He had only been in the car 15 minutes or so, but the warmth from the heater combined with his daydreaming had made him forget how bitterly cold it was outside. Pushing his hands deep into his overcoat pockets he felt a piece of paper; it must be what the security guard in the car had done. Looking around at the guards, he was unable to tell which one might have placed it there. Frustrated that his normally good memory was failing him, and slightly irritated with himself for not paying more attention at the time, he decided to investigate it a bit further.

He glanced around to check if any of the guards were looking at him and as they seemed preoccupied with their own conversations, he quickly pulled out the paper. Slowly he opened it, trying to be quiet and secretly enjoying the 'James Bond' feel of the situation. He quickly read the words and put it back in his pocket, unaware that one of the guards had seen him. Short and to the point, it read 'GO TO THE BATHROOM'.

He was a bit surprised, as he hadn't actually been told to go to the bathroom since he was about six years old but decided to obey anyway.

"Anything we should know about, Mr President?"

"NO!" he snapped quickly. Realising he might give the game away, he hastily added in a much calmer tone,

"I … mean … it's just a note from my wife. You know how wives are …"

"Yeah, do I ever … You know Mr President, my wife always …"

"Are you okay, Mr President?" interrupted another one of the guards, "You don't look so good, Sir."

Gerry McQuillan was starting to feel quite anxious and nauseous about the whole thing.

"I'll be okay ... but I just need a couple of minutes. If you'll excuse me ..."

"Yeah, no problem, but I think someone should go with you ... just to be safe."

"I'll take him ... You guys keep a look out outside."

There was a lot of nodding and mumbling, followed by Gerry McQuillan being escorted to the toilet by one of the security guards. He tried protesting that he would be fine alone, but as he was feeling quite nauseous it turned out to be a pretty feeble protest.

He was, however, a bit concerned that the presence of the guard might ruin things. Not that he knew what to expect anyway.

"I'd use cubicle one if I were you, Sir. It's usually cleaner."

He tried to focus on the security guard, but his head was spinning too much to see straight.

"I'll just make sure those guys are still outside."

This all seemed a bit much to take in and, trying desperately to compose himself, he pushed open the door to cubicle one. Inside sat a man who looked very similar to the President. Not completely identical: not alike enough to fool Nina, but certainly close enough to get past a handful of security guards.

"Swap clothes," whispered the man.

Gerry obeyed, noticing that not only did he look like him, but the man's movements were pretty much identical to his own.

"Did Luc send you?"

"Who?"

Gerry McQuillan sighed, after all, it was the answer he had expected. He'd have to do better than that if he was going to get any idea what to expect.

"Well, okay, but do you have a name?"

"Yes," smiled the man, "Gerry McQuillan."

"Of course."

As soon as they had made the swap, the man went to leave.

"Before you go ... what happens next?"

"You'll see." and with that, he was gone.

He sat down on the toilet seat, he could hear the security guards outside asking *him* if he felt better and he could also hear *himself* answering them. It was a very peculiar feeling and one he definitely wasn't in any hurry to repeat. He listened as the footsteps and voices gradually faded. He heard the plane's engines, the sound of take-off, and then—silence. An all-consuming, horrifyingly unnerving silence. Now he was afraid, and his fear was reflected in his thoughts.

What if he was being kidnapped by terrorists?

What if Luc wasn't real?

What if nobody came for him?

How exactly would he explain why the most powerful man in the world was sat on the john at a disused airfield, all alone? Worse than that would be having to explain exactly why he had handed his clothes and jewellery over to a man he had never before set eyes on. Without even being threatened.

After what seemed like ages to Gerry but was, in reality, only about five or ten minutes, he heard footsteps. He prayed that they were friendly, but his mind had ideas of its own and was determined to go through a lot more 'What if' scenarios. The footsteps grew louder and were obviously getting closer. Now he was more afraid than ever and sat tight, trying not to breathe too loudly for fear the steps were hostile. Inside the cubicle, Gerry cowered slightly as he heard the door being pushed open.

"Gerry? ... Are you there? ... Gerry"

He tried to answer but no sound came out. Then the cubicle door opened.

In front of him stood a shadowy figure, whose appearance was enough to unnerve even the most decorated member of the U.S. Special Forces. He was dressed from head to foot in black combat-style clothing, complete with balaclava and dark glasses; he was also packing what appeared to be a very lethal sci-fi death ray-gun. A very nervous Gerry McQuillan assumed it must be a prototype of some description. More than anything else, he hoped that whatever it was, it wasn't about to be used on him.

"Shall we go then, Sir?" the figure asked in a soft, almost musical voice.

"Oh ... hmm ... yes ... I suppose so."

He couldn't really tell what gender the person was: the build was male, but the voice was definitely female. He thought it was probably female, because men that sounded that much like women weren't generally considered combat material. He decided not to think about it too much as, if the rest of the day was anything to go by, they could be either, neither, or both.

Male, female, androgynous, or hermaphrodite. Whatever they were, he followed them out onto the airfield. Only a few feet away was a triangular shape he presumed must be an aircraft. Either it was another prototype, or he *was* being abducted by aliens. He rubbed his eyes, assuming he was tired and possibly dreaming, but it was still there; he actually went as far as pinching himself, just to double check. It was real, and he could feel his stomach begin to churn. He desperately hoped the stories about alien probes and implants weren't true.

The only reassurance came from the figure's soft, feminine voice.

"It's all right Gerry, you're safe ... Just stay with me, okay?"

He nodded. He wasn't likely to do anything else at the moment.

Looking along the aircraft, if indeed it *was* an aircraft, he saw there were no markings, no windows, and no visible door. It was a completely smooth, metal, triangular prism. There were no visible lights of any sort, and the craft itself was not a bright, shiny, metallic object. In fact, against the icy purple-grey sky it was completely camouflaged. If he had been any further away, he would not have been able to see it at all.

It seemed strange even to Gerry how, despite the sheer terror that washed over him, he couldn't help but feel slightly in awe of whoever had created it.

As they reached the craft, a slit appeared in the side reminding him of every science-fiction film he had ever watched. However, unlike a film, there was no bright green, glowing light beaming out of the slit. From a distance, the door opening would be no more noticeable than the rest of the craft.

Once inside, the slit closed behind him. There was nothing inside to suggest the thing could even move, let alone fly: no flashy controls, spotlights, strip-lights, or computers. The walls inside were as smooth as the outside: not a trace of a 1950s flying-saucer egg-box interior anywhere. The only light was an ambient lilac glow that filled the whole craft. Eleven deep purple reclining chair-beds, arranged in a circle, were situated at the centre of the craft. These were currently occupied by sleeping world leaders; he correctly assumed that the empty one was for him.

As he lay down, he felt his body sink into the soft chair-bed. After all the emotional turmoil he had been through, he was at last beginning to feel relaxed. He sensed a pleasant aroma which, he figured, based on the sleeping Premiers, must be either an anaesthetic or tranquiliser. As the scent filled the room, the figure gently strapped him in.

"Who are you?" He asked in a sleepy voice.

"I'm a Ghost."

"Uuh ... U ... u ... h ..."

With that he was asleep.

The next thing he was aware of was being woken up by the soft-spoken Ghost.

"Wake up Gerry. It's time to go ... we're here."

He yawned, rubbed his eyes sleepily, and gazed around. The room was still lilac, so he obviously hadn't dreamt it all. He went to look at his watch and remembered how he had handed it to the substitute Gerry McQuillan in the restroom.

"How long have I been asleep? ... I mean what time is it?"

"You people worry too much about time ... You shouldn't, it's not important ... What's important is why you're here."

"*Why* am I here?"

"To see Luc, of course."

"Who is he? ... Luc, I mean."

"You'll see."

This was unknown territory to any politician, normally they are as forewarned and forearmed as is humanly possible. This time, however, it seemed impossible to gain any information about anything. He tried a different approach.

"What's your name?" he asked.

"I don't have a name, I'm a Ghost."

"Don't ghosts have names then? I thought everything had a name."

"No, not everything. Some things don't have names and I'm just one of those things."

"Oh." was the best he could manage, realising that he wasn't going to learn anything no matter what tactic he used. At least, if nothing else, he now knew that he was going to see Luc and not be abducted by probing aliens.

Outside the craft, the light was pale blue and much brighter. The air was warm and although he knew they were inside, it reminded him of a warm summer day. Something America had not seen since the Yellowstone eruption.

The aircraft was now also pale blue, and once again perfectly camouflaged. He marvelled at the craft and wondered at the technology involved in it. He decided that if Luc was responsible in any way for the creation of such a craft, then he must be a genius. He also briefly considered the possibility of the aircraft being connected to the Roswell incident; this was followed by the idea that Luc may have been a surviving crash victim from Roswell.
Fortunately for Gerry's deep-fried brain, a door opened behind him.

"Come on Gerry. Its time."

The Ghost gestured towards the door and Gerry, now much calmer, followed the other world leaders through it. He hadn't seen the door until it opened, but it didn't come as any surprise that there was one, or that there was a lift behind it. At least, he assumed it was a lift and they hadn't all just been herded into a cupboard. Once the doors closed, he and the other leaders were on their own. There was an uncomfortable silence for a moment, then came a more familiar voice:

"Don't worry, everything is fine. It's actually going to be a real eye- opener for you all. Luc is really a quite ... fascinating individual. We'll soon be ... sorry ... my mistake ...We *are* moving."

The voice was that of the very well-spoken Crown Prince Ghazal, who was the only person there who had ever met Luc before. His English was absolutely perfect, and he was right, they were moving. Not up or down, but horizontally.

Oh well. It's different. thought Gerry to himself, becoming resigned to the peculiarity of the situation.

Various members of the group tried interrogating the Prince, largely as to why they had been chosen, but he reasoned it wasn't worth trying to explain anything when they only had seconds until they would meet Luc face to face.

The lift slowed; Gerry felt more at ease, naively assuming nothing else could shock him, and was beginning to rekindle his earlier enthusiasm at the idea of meeting the geriatric genius. The time from the lift slowing down to it actually stopping seemed the longest part of the day. Looking around at the others, he could see the anticipation on their faces too. Up until now, it had all been very surreal and he was itching to meet the man responsible.

When the lift did eventually stop, the doors opened, and they were greeted by a young man.

The man appeared to be in his late twenties. His long, fair hair was tied neatly back in a plait and his skin was sun-tanned, yet western in appearance. His eyes were incredibly dark. Gerry thought they actually looked black, but as it had been a long day he decided they were probably just a very deep brown.
He wore white Karate trousers with a long, open white coat that almost reached the ground. He wore nothing under the coat, and no shoes.

Gerry couldn't help but feel this was a strange dress code, but as nothing about Luc appeared to be conventional, why would his staff be any different?

"Welcome," said the man with the same soft musical tones as the Ghost.

"I am Luc."

CHAPTER 7

From the lift doorway the Saudi Prince was the first to speak:

"It is an honour and a pleasure to be here again, and I thank you."

The others, who were still dazed from the journey, watched as the Prince removed his shoes and socks and stepped out of the lift onto the soft white carpet. Luc smiled: a warm safe smile.

"Honestly, Ghazal. I can assure you the pleasure is as much mine as it is yours. Now, I would be very honoured if the rest of you would remove your footwear and come into my house."

They filed out of the lift, dutifully removing their shoes and, if they were wearing any, their socks as Luc continued with his introductory speech. The British Premier was just relieved that she had worn trousers.

"We have much to discuss and I feel sure that you must have many questions yourselves. I will endeavour to answer all of them later. First though, I have prepared food as I am sure you must be hungry." They followed him down the hallway.

"In my house you will notice there are no clocks. Time is just a countdown from birth to death. While you are here there is no need to be concerned with it; likewise, newspapers or bulletins ... they are depressing at best. Here, for a while, you are free from the day-to-day constraints and pressures of office. Here, I address important issues in a less formal ... more relaxed ... and, I like to think, more civilised manner than the meetings you are all used to."

As they followed Luc down the hallway they passed several thick wooden doors, with crystal knobs and hinges that sparkled like diamonds. They were as curious as they were decorative. The clean white walls were dotted with several architectural drawings of great wonders from the ancient world.

"Ah, I see you are admiring my drawings."

"Did you draw them?" asked the Australian Prime Minister, gesturing towards what resembled a blueprint of the sphinx. Luc laughed.

"One good thing about Australians ... They're never lost for words for long, eh?"

Steve Cooper managed a sheepish smile as everyone grinned at him.

"Anyway ... Yes, an old friend and I did them a long time ago. We thought it would be a fun project ... It was ..."

Luc had a faraway look,

"... But that was a long time ago. Where was I? Ah yes, while you are here you may speak to me in your native tongue, as I am fluent in all your languages and dialects. I suspect English is preferable for you all; however, for anyone who cannot speak English I am willing to translate."

They reached the room at the end of the hall.

"This is the dining room. Sit wherever you feel comfortable. There is wine ... white or red, or there is water; I am afraid that is all I drink, but there is plenty of it." He smiled. The smile broadened to a grin as he added, "King Arthur's table," and gestured towards a large round table holding a buffet which was sumptuous, even by world leaders' standards.

Around the table were white leather armchairs the height of dining chairs; this made eating a very comfortable and relaxing experience. Gerry McQuillan was at last starting to feel more at ease with the situation. If it turned out that he had been abducted by aliens, at least they provided a good meal before doing any nasty probing or experiments. Curious about their host he, too, decided to try an art question; after all, it had worked for the Aussie P.M.

"Ex … excuse me … Luc. I was … er … wondering … about … er … that picture. I mean … It looks very old."

He was pointing towards what had once been a very colourful caricature, but now appeared somewhat faded with time.

"Mmm, good choice, Gerry … it's a favourite of mine." Luc smiled at the President, and Gerry knew that Luc knew that he was only making small talk to assess the safety of the situation. Luc however wasn't about unnerving people; he wanted them to feel comfortable around him and it *was* one of his favourites, so he was happy to talk about it. Armed with a half-eaten chicken leg, he launched enthusiastically into an ancient art appreciation lesson:

"'Apelles' Calumny,' or when Botticelli painted his version, 'The Calumny of Apelles'. Can't say as I was struck on Botticelli's version." He shook his head, frowning slightly.

"I feel this is much closer to the painting described by Lucian, with more satirical impact." He could see his guests looked a little puzzled and continued to elaborate further:

"Lucian was apparently an ancient Syrian. I say 'apparently', as I don't think anyone really knows his origins. He was a satirist. Therefore, it seems reasonable that if Lucian bothered to mention Apelles' work, it must be because of the satirical content. Botticelli's version is far too ... acceptable. Yes, that's the right word ... acceptable, and perhaps *too* profound."

He looked around and as they all seemed interested, he continued, taking a rare opportunity to, as he viewed it, set the record straight:

"You see, in this version ..." he said, gesturing towards the painting with the still half-eaten chicken leg ... "how the man has elephant's ears so he can clearly hear the voices of the hags who represent Ignorance and Suspicion. On the other side of him, this twisted man is Envy, followed by the beautiful False Accusation or Calumny. She, in turn, is aided and abetted by Treachery and Fraud. Here, following behind, we see Penitence tearing at her hair, with cuts on her face ... a Greek tradition of women in mourning was to tear at their hair and cut their faces. And finally, comes Truth. The innocent- looking youth you see being dragged along is actually himself ... Apelles."

He laughed, noting the odd confused expression among his guests.

"The artist was reputed to have painted this after he was accused of being a conspirator by a jealous artist in King Ptolemy's court; so you see, it was nothing more than a newspaper-style cartoon, having a dig at the stupidity of their government or, in this case, the King."

Now they were hooked. Luc's personality and way of seeing things made it very hard not to admire him, and boring certainly wasn't a quality he could be accused of.

"Who painted this one?" asked Gerry, suddenly wanting to know more.

"The signature is so faded with age it's impossible to say." Luc had taken note of the fact that they had finished eating while he had been speaking.

"Anyway, I think it is time for more important matters." Replacing the chicken leg on the plate he added, "Follow me to the lounge … It is a more comfortable place to discuss things."

Gerry thought it seemed strange that there had been no language confusion during Luc's art lesson. He felt sure that not all the other guests spoke English that well. He remembered how Luc had said he was fluent in all their languages, but even Luc couldn't speak in several different languages at the same time … could he? Once inside the lounge, Gerry gave up worrying about it.

"Please sit down wherever you feel most comfortable."

There was the same deep white carpet that ran throughout Luc's home, large white leather chairs, big soft floor cushions, small tables with wine carafes, water jugs, beautiful gold-rimmed goblets, and more paintings and strange ornaments.

Pope Gregory caught sight of a polished wooden box, which had a winged lion with a human head situated at each end. There were four legs on the box and poles either side of it, presumably for carrying. He assumed it must be a replica of the Ark of the Covenant.

"I cannot help but notice Luc, that you have a lot of religious artefacts."

"Ah, Richard ..."

This shocked everyone else—nobody ever called the Pope by his real name.

"I see you all look shocked. I must apologise. In my house there are no titles or surnames, just the first names you were born with. Except, of course should you have been adopted, I am happy to use the name your adoptive parents gave you."

"Do *you* not have a surname, or family name?" The Pope asked.

"I do not even have a family, so how could I have a family name? I will explain now, to save time later: I never knew my parents; myself and my sister, Li-Li, were brought up by people who we thought were our friends. Then one day my sister married; she was married for only a few days and after that I never saw her again. I do not know where she went or even what happened to her; she just vanished. I left and never went back. For a while I looked for Li-Li, but eventually I gave up searching and because of this, I never married or had children. The pain of losing one person is enough."

"That's awful." Priyanka looked genuinely moved.

Luc butted in before she could add anything else.

"As I was saying before my life story," he began, turning his attention once again to the Pope, "I have as many non-religious artefacts as I do religious ones. Likewise, I have as many gadgets and gismos as I do artefacts."

The Pope looked a bit put out by this but realised, looking around, that Luc was right: there were no more religious items than there were purely cultural ones. There was a brief unsure silence as everyone looked around the room, trying to take in their surroundings.

"Now," began Luc, "Fire away … Ask me your questions and I will, as I said earlier, endeavour to answer them."

They looked at each other, wondering what questions they should ask.

"Why are we here?" demanded the Russian President eventually.

"Good question, Felix." replied Luc. "As I am sure you are all aware from the microchip, the Earth is destined to be hit by a meteor in 2055. As you also know, there are children in your countries who are mankind's future ... I speak, of course, of the ones in the secret facilities. You are here now because you are the last world leaders who I shall have any dealings with." He paused to take a sip of his water; his expression was now showing signs of melancholy.

"You are currently leading your countries in a post-apocalyptic world. There will be very few elections between now and 2055; therefore, you have much work to do, and you will have more meetings with me before the end."

"Will anybody survive this meteor ... I mean on this planet?" asked the Indian Prime Minister, Priyanka Joshi, tentatively. She and Ella Jameson were the only women present.

"I am so sorry, but no."

"But ... is there nothing we can do?"

"I am truly sorry, Priyanka. If there was anything, I would tell you, I promise. I understand that being female, you and Ella feel this differently to anyone else, but we are doing the only thing we can. Try and take comfort in the fact that you are at least saving humanity."

"What about you? ... Will you go too?"

"No, Tian. I am not going ... My place is here. These children have been raised for this and I haven't; my destiny is with you, here on the planet."

"What if we want to leave with the children?"

"I am sorry. I understand your fear Ella but, like me, you are not prepared for a new world. They are."

"What about everyone else? There will be chaos. What are we s'posed to do about that, eh?"

"This is a valid point. Thank you for making it."

He glanced appreciatively towards the Australian, relieved for a minute that somebody had something less emotive to offer.

"The way I see it, there are two choices: one is to say nothing, but the likelihood is an astronomer would let the cat out of the bag; the other is to hold a lottery to see who goes. It would, of course, be a dummy lottery, but it may give hope ..."

"But false hope," Gerry McQuillan interrupted. "Is that not crueller?"

"I do not know, Gerry. I do not have the answer, but if anybody else has better suggestions I'm willing to listen."

There were, of course, several options put forward for dealing with an 'end of the world' situation, all of which Luc already knew, but like any good diplomat, he wanted them to make the final decisions. He was, after all was said and done, giving them eight years to come up with an overall game plan for controlling the masses.

"What about children? The ones from America ... are they even still alive after everything that has happened there?" Everyone looked towards Gerry for the answer; he felt very uncomfortable as he muttered,

"I ... Truthfully, I don't know."

"I do." answered Luc. "Fortunately for Gerry, I managed to move the children out of Area 51. And actually Eitan, seeing as you asked, they are in Israel. But you couldn't have known that Gerry ... It was very quick."

"I feel so bad; you know ... about Peggy. I should've listened to her."

"I know ... she had a brilliant mind, but she always was a little *too* obsessed. A volcano would've got her sooner or later anyway."

Gerry wasn't entirely sure whether he was supposed to find that reassuring or not. He did, however, feel relieved about the children from Area 51. Area 51 was a multi-layered facility and deep within the facility lay the real purpose behind it: the children that were to be the future of humankind. These children would leave the planet just before the meteor was expected to destroy it and make a new 'Earth' on Mars.

Mars, itself, was already undergoing a climate change, so using large thermal heaters and bacteria should accelerate the process of 'terra forming'.

The next level of the hidden facilities, beneath the surface, housed spaceships like the one they travelled in to see Luc. These were built by Ghosts. Nobody knew that these other levels existed in the secret facilities other than those involved in the project. And even then only they knew very little. Everything was always on 'a need to know' basis.' The top level was used by the military, to conduct secret experiments involving aircraft and weapons. The various prototype planes gave rise to the belief that aliens, or alien technology was present within these areas. This was very handy, as people just assumed that was what the Governments were hiding and combined with the military's right to protect its own secrets by shooting trespassers, it meant nobody would ever discover the truth.

"What are the children like?"

"Only a mother would ask such a question wouldn't you say, Priyanka?"

"Maybe, but I would like to know anyway; if that's okay?"

"I'd like to know *whose* children they are ... I mean, who their parents are. I think we're all a little bit curious about that."

Everyone nodded and mumbled agreement. Gerry felt very proud that he'd asked the right question, and Priyanka felt very relieved that for the moment she had lost the spotlight.

"I will explain as best I can. The children themselves are a mixture of absolutely brilliant-minded scientists, architects, and engineers, and a work force. I have tried to maintain a balance, creating 30% of the children as geniuses and 70% as manual workers. It may have worked better with an 80 – 20% ratio, but I wanted everyone to be the crème-de-la-creme of their profession. So, the 10 –15% not quite brilliant, but not daft either, who are present in most societies, in this society became geniuses."

"As you all know, designing babies is relatively common and the procedure is simple. We have added a few other modifications to the usual process: first, the children were created using frozen sperm and embryos from scientific geniuses, expert craftsmen, and/or the super-fit. The test-tube embryos were then placed in surrogate host mothers who were unrelated to them; growing babies outside of a human is still very much a vision of the future. The only other difference was a few adjustments made to the ageing gene to retard the ageing process, therefore allowing them to produce more children themselves. I am sure it has not escaped your notice that I, myself, look much younger than I actually am. This is because I became the laboratory rat for this process. The reason it has not found its way into medicine yet is because, apart from the children, I am the only other human it has been tested on. Therefore, side-effects are as yet unknown."

"Is that safe? What if it goes wrong?"

"Truthfully, I do not know. Thus far I have been all right so I can only assume it is safe, but I have no idea what the long-term effects might be, should it turn out to have any. There is a valid reason for needing them to live longer: there are only a few of them, so they need to have as many children as they can. But you must also remember that these children do not have families of their own, so they will need time between children to adjust to parenthood. Anyway, where was I? Ah, yes ... I was saying that the host mothers lived within the facility until the children were born ... mostly they were multiple births ... between three and five children per birth. Once the children were born, the mothers were re-housed and given a large settlement. Oh ... and of course, their memories were erased."

"Does that hurt? Having your memory erased?"

"Certainly not. It is a very simple and totally painless process."

It was actually a question most of them would've liked to ask but didn't, in case it made them look stupid; nonetheless, Gerry felt a bit of an idiot because he had done so well with his last comment.

"Let me just get this straight ..." began Steve Cooper, "These children ... they've got Einstein for their dad and Miss World as their mum?"

"Don't be daft!" snapped Ella. "He just said they were geniuses, not airheads. It's like Einstein as your dad and Marie Curie as your mum."

"Exactly." finished Luc.

"Well, I liked my idea better. Eh, boys?"

The Australian was, in reality, neither as daft nor as brash as he appeared, but he *was* quite amusing.

"Anyway," said Luc, bringing things back to order. "The children have been, and for that matter are still being, educated within the facilities. Obviously, those who teach them are not only geniuses, but are also the parents of some of the children, although for security reasons neither the teachers nor the children are aware of that. The teachers never leave the facilities, and it is very unlikely they ever will. Their education involves the usual curriculum, with religious education removed. This includes all forms of religion, not just those considered mainstream."

"It does seem wrong to me to have no belief …"

"I understand that it seems that way to you, Richard, but you are not the only one in this room with a belief. For example, while you believe in Catholicism, Ghazal is devoutly Muslim, and Akil has a country divided between the two. Priyanka is Hindu, whilst Arubel is Greek orthodox. Whose religion should we teach? And if we teach all of them … well, it's just something else that can cause conflicts and eventually wars. Too many people have died on this planet in the name of their God—do any of us really want that to happen again?"

The Pope took a last-ditch attempt at making Luc see the need for a religion:

"Do you not have any religious beliefs yourself, Luc?"

"I have beliefs about religion; I also have beliefs about a lot of things. Mostly, I believe any religion can be dangerous. A true belief is as dangerous in the wrong hands as a false belief is in the right hands."

Richard rolled his eyes; it was the sort of ambiguous answer he had expected, and the best answer he was going to get.

"It is true ... my country has been divided over its religious beliefs for a very long time and although I am Muslim, I know that in the past the Christians suffered mercilessly at the hands of the Muslims. I do not wish to see that repeated anywhere." This was the first time Akil had spoken, and he may not speak a lot, but the little he *does* say certainly has an impact. Generally, it was agreed that the state of the world didn't suggest religious education to be the best idea, but morals did need to be taught.

"Just because we are not teaching religion does not mean we are not teaching any morals or offering any spiritual guidance. But we shall go into that later, as I have somebody else arriving who I would prefer to discuss this subject with you."

Luc glanced quickly around the room, ensuring that everyone was once again looking comfortable after the heated subject of religion.

"Anyway, I have planned for the children to leave and travel to Mars in larger versions of the ship you all arrived in."

"How exactly does that ship work?"

"I cannot tell you that, for obvious reasons; were I to hand over that information, any military organisation would instantly pounce on it. It is, after all, the ultimate in stealth technology. It is also, like all the prototypes I possess, safer in my hands."

"There must be good things we could do with it?"

"Felix, my friend, I understand your curiosity and of course it can be used for good things, but it never seems to turn out that way. Humankind, as a whole, is neither enlightened nor advanced enough to cope with it. I am sure you understand; besides, *we* are doing something good with it: we are, in case you had forgotten, using it to save the human race from extinction."

"You speak of mankind as though ..."

He stopped to reconsider the question. It was the first time the Greek president had contributed to the conversation, and obviously he was not too sure that he should have bothered at all.

"As though what, Arubel? Do continue ... Please."

"As though ... you are not ... well ... one of them." Arubel could feel everyone looking at him, but there was no going back; he'd said it now.

"If I am not a man ... or indeed, even a human ... then what might I be? Do you have any ideas? If so, please share them." Luc's attention was now fixed on Arubel. Yet his smiling, almost wicked expression let everyone, including Arubel, know that he was only playing with him.

"For the record, I am as human as you are ... unless ..." he hesitated, looked around the room at the anticipation on their faces,

"... unless, of course, there are any of you that are not human?"

They managed a stifled laugh, as they realised the lunacy of being relieved that their host was human. After all, he certainly, looked and, for that matter, behaved like a human.

"Are the Ghosts human too?" Ella whispered, fearing she might also be asking an incredibly stupid question. She had a bit of a reputation for being 'Britain's dumb blonde Prime Minister'. She wasn't, but she was probably the most attractive Premier and as everyone knows, pretty, clever women don't exist, and certainly not in politics. She hurriedly amended her question:

"What I mean is ... Who are they?"

"Well, actually ..." said Luc, smirking, obviously getting a great deal of amusement out this question, "... they're not human." The smirking now progressed to laughing, as he particularly enjoyed the confusion written in capital letters across their faces. "They're holograms."

"How can they be? I mean ... they are solid. That's not possible." Gerry was as baffled as the rest of them, and his curiosity had long since overridden his nerves.

"I am sorry Ella; I wasn't laughing at you ... just at the situation. I hope you are not offended; I really wouldn't want to offend any of you. And yes, Gerry, technically it's not possible ... or at least it *wasn't*. Let me explain presumably you know that a three-dimensional hologram *can* be produced using electronics, white light-emitting diodes, and fibre optics.

This is not new, the Japanese perfected it earlier this century."

They all nodded knowingly, most of them not actually having the faintest idea what he was talking about but at least making an effort to look like they did.

"... You most probably also know about entangled pairs ... a quantum physics idea ... and the fact that these elementary particles have an ability to communicate with each other. It is just a case of finding out what frequencies they respond to, then if we can zap them with the right frequency ..."

He could see they were completely lost despite their feeble attempts to hide their cluelessness. He decided it was probably best to quickly conclude this particular monologue before baffling them any further.

"... they will separate away from their holographic state to become solid. That's basically it, in a nutshell. Of course, to make them function in the same way as the Ghosts you need a little more ... technical wizardry and quantum hocus-pocus."

Gerry was still curious and wanted to find out more about the man, as opposed to his technical ability. After all, nobody in the room apart from Luc had any real idea how to create a basic hologram, let alone one that could fly a spaceship.

"Is that what you do then? Advanced technology?"

"I *think* ... I *believe* that with enough thought, you can create anything; after all, nothing can be invented without putting some thought behind it. I do develop prototypes, but I tend to keep hold of any that can be used for the destruction of man. That way, the world is a bit safer—maybe Einstein and Oppenheimer should have thought about safety too. I concede that somebody would've still split the atom one day, but maybe it could have waited until mankind was a bit more responsible. Still ... Let he who is without sin ... etcetera."

They conceded that was a fair point, but Gerry still had more questions.

"Well ... Okay. I understand that the world is unsafe, and you say that you're not prepared to help us destroy ourselves but ... well ... what about the guns the Ghosts carry? They could destroy us, couldn't they?"

"*No, they couldn't.* They're tranquilisers: all they would do is make you fall asleep. Besides which, Ghosts only use them for defence—*never for attack.*"

Gerry thought it might be a good time to be quiet and let someone else have a go at looking a twit!

"I don't know about you, but I feel we have covered quite a lot of ground. And we have certainly learnt more about each other. I know you still have a lot of questions, but I think we could all do with a rest. Come, I will show you to your rooms; you can freshen up and get some sleep."

They followed him back through the dining room, where the table was now clear, and back down the corridor towards the lift. The doors they had passed when they came in were the doors to their rooms. Luc opened the first door.

"Priyanka, this is your apartment; the interior door connects with the apartment next door. I have prepared that one for Ella; I know how women like company." They seemed pleased with that arrangement.

"You can lock the connecting door if you want privacy. I will see you later."

"Are all these doors to apartments?" asked the Australian.

"In my house there are many mansions," he replied.

Ghazal smiled, he quite liked Luc's occasional mildly blasphemous digs. It was a relief after the confines of his strict

Muslim upbringing. The Pope, however, did not look so amused but he was too tired to get into another religious battle.

He continued along the corridor showing the men to their rooms. It was all a bit more familiar now but probably they all noticed there was no sign of the lift doors and thought it a little strange. No one actually said anything though, most of them just assumed the lift must be a secret panel.

Their apartments had the same white carpet and soft lighting that was present in the rest of the house. It wasn't dim lighting, just soft—easily light enough to see by—but far more comfortable on the eyes. It felt like daylight and helped to mask the fact that there were no visible windows.

Gerry took stock of his surroundings and noticed a large round sunken area; which he assumed must be a type of Jacuzzi bath. Everything was as plush and comfortable, and white as was the rest of the house. Despite the fact that the bath looked really tempting he opted for a shower in case he fell asleep in the bath, something he was quite an expert in doing. Past experience had taught him the falling asleep bit was fine, it was the waking up in freezing cold water that was horrible.

Feeling much cleaner, he lay on the bed and tried to organise his thoughts on the events of the last few hours.

'So'. He thought to himself. 'The look-alike in the toilet, highly advanced holograms, the ultimate stealth spaceship, strange paintings, and artefacts, technical genius, and Luc ... a man who appears 50 years younger than he should, with no family and no religion. God only knows who he is.' His thoughts wandered for a moment. 'God? No Luc couldn't be God. Could he?' After all, he didn't appear anywhere near as old as he should be. No, not possible. Surely God would seem more omnipotent with less technical stuff and a more booming voice. God would also be far more religious, quite incensed, he imagined, at the idea of the children not being taught that *he* was the one true God.

Then there were the white carpet and walls throughout Luc's home. Gerry smiled to himself at the thought of how he had come from one White House to another. And now, at the end of what had been a very complex day, he found himself in the plushest suite of rooms he'd ever set foot in—better than any 5-star hotel.

Admittedly, he hadn't been able to find the light switch, but he was so tired he figured he could probably sleep regardless of the light. His thoughts were not getting any clearer, but he was getting sleepier. As his eyes closed, the light grew comfortably dimmer.

CHAPTER 8

On waking, Gerry McQuillan joined the others in the dining room where breakfast had already been prepared for them. At least, they assumed it was breakfast based on that being the meal generally eaten after sleep.

"It might just be me ... but did anyone notice anything ... well ... strange last night? About the lights, I mean."

Ella stopped in mid-sentence, considering whether it may just have been tiredness playing tricks on her.

"They faded as your eyes closed. Is that what you mean?"

"Yes, That's it!" She breathed a sigh of relief, grateful to Gerry for the reassurance.

"It was nice enough. Just a bit unusual ... but so is everything else here." She looked at Gerry for further confirmation, but he was too busy eating.

"I have to admit, I find it all a bit ...well ... comfortably strange."

"Yes, that's it! Comfortably strange. Well put, Arubel."

"I like it here and I like Luc. I find him good company and the best host I have ever met." Ghazal had just laid himself open for a hundred and one questions, most of them fairly trivial.

"Do you know who the other guest is?"

"Was it like this last time?"

"What else can we expect?"

Eventually it was Ella who came up with the "Ghazal, do you believe we can trust him?" question.

"Firstly, I don't know who this other guest is. I do however suspect that he or *she* must be pretty important to Luc; otherwise, he or *she* wouldn't be here. Secondly, Luc is actually more forthcoming this time and I think this must be because, like he said, we are the last people who will meet him. Obviously he believes that *The End* is imminent ... eight years isn't very long." He sighed before continuing,

"That sort of information is a lot of responsibility ... and Luc has had that responsibility for longer than any of us ... so ... Yes, I believe we can trust him."

"I suppose at least he is trying to do something good ... but I can't help but feel he is ... economical with the truth at times."

Ella couldn't help laughing at Gerry's last comment.

"We're politicians for Christ's sake. Every one of us is economical with the truth; that hardly makes us bad people ... or bad politicians for that matter."

Luc's arrival at the breakfast table instantly brought a halt to their discussion. He had deliberately arrived late to allow them the chance to talk among themselves. He understood that some, if not all of them were unsure about either him, the project, or both, and he was also relying on Ghazal to put their minds at rest. Luc hadn't been *listening* in to their conversation; he didn't need to. He would be able to tell if they were more relaxed or not by reading their body language.

Despite his earlier comment, Gerry did trust Luc. For a start, he understood the need to save his own species and he knew it would be a lot more difficult, if not impossible to achieve without Luc's help. Whilst it was true that he suspected there was more to Luc than he let on, he could also have said that about every one of the guests as well. Overall, he thought Luc was probably more honest than any of them would have been, given the same situation.

"I trust you are all more refreshed, as we have a lot more ground to cover before you return home."

Home, thought Gerry, *which* struck a chord. He hadn't given home a second thought since he was sat in the toilet at the airfield. He remembered Nina, his wife;

Jenny, his friend; and Ashley, his vice president, who was running the country in his absence; and the strange man at Camp David, who was standing in for him. He felt guilty at not having missed his wife when normally he would've done, particularly as he felt quite sure that she would be missing him. Inside the luxurious surroundings of Luc's home, the cold post-eruption world outside had ceased to exist.

"I have someone very special for you to meet soon, but I would like to clarify a few things beforehand. As you will no doubt recall, I said before that I had no wife or children. This is true … at least, I have no children of my own, but deciding *not to have* a family doesn't necessarily mean you *won't have* a family."

Gerry did remember him saying he had no family and had pretty much grasped the idea that this was a conscious decision on his part. After all, he and Nina had no children which was very unusual in a world where 'test-tube' babies were a common phenomenon. He also remembered the criticism they had endured from friends and family for not having any children—especially Nina's mother.

"I will explain." Luc continued. His voice forced Gerry to return from his 'guilt trip'.

"Twenty years ago, on one of my many inspection visits to the secret facilities I went to the Israeli facility. The workers had found a little boy, hiding under a table in the physics lab. They were confused because there was no possible way the child could've got in there. As I said earlier, they are multi-layered. It is unlikely that anyone, even a small child, could get past the top layer; they would certainly be apprehended by the second layer. Just to further clarify this point: there are no air ducts or pipes through which he could've crawled; besides which, the door to the physics lab was still secure. The only way in is a retina scan ... subsequently no one ever did discover how the child got there."

"Could an employee have put him there?" asked Ella, cringing as she remembered him saying that the employees lived within the facility.

"No, not at all. The employees never leave the facility, and we considered all options at the time. Even stranger was the fact that he had asked for me by name. As you are all aware ... as I'm sure you have all tried ..." He had a broad grin on his face as he continued, "I am impossible to track down. If those who have met me and those who I contact can't prove I exist, how could a small child have heard of me? Anyway, when I saw the boy he called me by name. I saw then that he had a small tattoo: the same as one my sister had. I don't know if he is Li-Li's son, but I know she must've had *something* to do with him. Sadly, when I asked him he couldn't remember; all he knew was to ask for me. It seemed that fate had intervened; that somehow my ... destiny was to look after this child, so that is what happened. He is the closest thing I have to a family."

"And the closest thing to your sister."

"Yes, Priyanka. How shrewd you can be. But you are right: he is the closest thing I have to my sister and that alone would make him very special." It was obvious to everyone watching Luc speak that he loved this boy as if he were his own son.

"I taught him all I know, and he too is a quantum physicist and works within the facilities as does his wife. Yes, he is married: she is a medical researcher and microbiologist in the Egyptian facility."

"Do they have children?"

"No Gerry, like you and I, they decided not to. Unlike us though, theirs is self-sacrificing. There is much work to be done with the children so they are going with them as they will be needed there."

He paused, waiting for the protests; he knew it was a provocative statement. He was right: there were a few complaints about *his* child going when *theirs* wouldn't, and several comments about how escaping a doomed planet wasn't exactly 'self-sacrificing'. After listening to a few of their objections, Luc decided he'd had enough and that this line of accusatory questioning wasn't at all productive.

"First," he said, with his voice slightly raised, so as to be heard, "Which one of your children can either design, build, or maintain a spacecraft like mine? Or create a Ghost? In fact, do any of your children even have a quantum physics higher qualification?"

There was an uncomfortable silence but no arguments.

"That's what I thought. You are all impressed by my technical abilities; well, my son's abilities are as good as mine, if not better. His wife will also be invaluable, but I will let him explain it to you. Please follow me."

They followed him back through to the lounge where his guest was waiting for them.

"I would like you to meet my son, Kabal."

CHAPTER 9

If Luc was beautiful, Kabal was even more so: he had flowing white hair, and pink eyes that shone. It was obvious to all that he was an albino, yet although his skin was pale he did not have the sickly washed-out appearance that is so common with albinism. In fact, if anything, his appearance was radiant.

Gerry drew the conclusion that the soft lighting must be because Kabal had an intolerance to bright light, a common problem for albinos.

"It is so wonderful to meet you." His voice was as soft and musical as Luc's.

"I know this has been a lot to take in and I hope I can clarify a few things for you."

He looked around, checking he had their undivided attention. His body language and mannerisms were identical to those of their host. In fact, Kabal, had he not been albino would have been a carbon copy of Luc. It was strange to think Kabal was only Luc's adopted son.

They all knew that Luc was at least fifty years older than he looked, but even bearing that in mind it was still a very surreal experience watching a man introduce his son when they both looked exactly the same age. They seemed far too close in age to be father and son, yet at the same time they were far too alike in appearance and behaviour to not be.

"I have worked closely with Luc on this project since I was old enough to help and I have learnt a great deal from him. Currently, I am teaching the children quantum physics; this includes the building and maintenance of spacecraft, Ghosts, and other technology. Also, I am, along with my wife providing the children with non-denominational moral guidance: basically, not stealing from others, showing respect to each other, etcetera."

"Like the 10 commandments?"

"Not exactly, Richard. For the purposes of a well-adjusted society with no religious beliefs, the first four of Moses' commandments are obsolete. The fifth is only valid in families where the child is shown honour and respect and besides, I cannot expect these children to honour their fathers and mothers when they don't actually have any ... or at least, none they are aware of. Also, the last commandment is vague. It is not necessarily unhealthy to desire that which your neighbour has ... but it may lead to problems depending on what form that desire takes. So, in that instance, it is a case of helping people to deal with their emotions positively.

I suppose if you really want to view it like Moses it would be the three, possibly four and a half commandments." He winked at the Pope, who just knew he was never going to win a religious argument in this house. Everyone smiled; Kabal was definitely Luc's flesh and blood.

"You mean, it's sort of ... the less rules there are, the less rules there are to break."

"I would prefer to view it as the more practical the rules are, the easier it is not to break them. For instance, Gerry, I cannot tell people it is a sin to feel greed, envy, or gluttony occasionally; they are human emotions. Helping them not to let these emotions grow out of control is more productive than trying to suppress them which can lead to far worse problems."

Everyone nodded, there was sense behind what Kabal said.

"I trust you understand some of what we are trying to achieve now, as I wish to discuss a more ... personal issue." He paused to take a breath and once again ensure everyone was listening.

"I understand that there is probably much resentment that I get to leave Earth while you and your families remain here. I do understand this, and I am sorry ... Luc brought me up to go with the children, as their mentor. If it were possible to take everyone then we would, but ... well ... it isn't. I have to leave Luc behind ... and that, for me, is devastating. For you ... you will, no doubt make arrangements to spend time with your families and will probably be with them at the end. Luc has done so much to help the human race continue yet he will be alone at the end. I am telling you this so that when you feel bitter, you can remember that the person who spent years ensuring that your race survives and continues will be left here alone, with no family and, once again, no recognition." He did not elaborate further, but there was definitely a hint of sadness in his voice.

    Gerry didn't feel as guilty as the others, but he did feel for Kabal. He could see that Kabal loved Luc like a father and obviously found the thought of leaving him behind painful, but all their feelings of guilt and remorse were cut short by Kabal's last sentence. They couldn't help but wonder exactly what else Luc had done before, for which he had received no recognition. Before anyone had a chance to probe into this any further, Luc appeared in the doorway. Up until then, no one had actually been aware that he had left the room.

"I am very sorry, but it is time for you to return. We will meet again soon; I promise."

There was a melancholy silence as they followed Luc down the hallway to the lift, which was once again visible.

"Until next time, my friends …"

With that, the lift closed, and they returned to their post-eruption world via the same route by which they had left it. Gerry knew that as pleasant as his time with Luc may have been, the information he had received there meant he now faced a new challenge.

CHAPTER 10

Gerry Mcquillan returned to the airfield, once again exchanging clothes with the stranger in the toilet where he had listened to the voices of the security guards outside. He was trying to pick out the voice of the security guard who had originally directed him to cubicle one. It was all far too much of a coincidence for Luc not to have been involved. It was a pretty pointless exercise, because however hard he tried he could neither recollect his voice nor his face. It was also very unlikely that the security guard had ever set eyes on Luc—even if Luc had employed him, Gerry felt sure it would probably have been very indirectly.

"Till next time," whispered the stranger, handing a small envelope to Gerry.

Although somewhat startled by this he knew there was a good chance that if he replied, the security guards would probably hear him. Knowing what they were like, they would either come rushing in to save him assuming there was a security breach or consider him mad for talking to himself. Neither was desirable, with the latter having a very real likelihood of becoming White House gossip that could have very unfavourable repercussions. Gerry picked the safest option: just nodding and smiling in acknowledgement as he left the cubicle to return home.

The drive back from the airfield to the White House seemed much shorter than it had on the outward journey and didn't really allow him anywhere near enough time to come to terms with the last couple of days. All he knew for certain was that he and his life had gone through a fairly dramatic metamorphosis. He could never be the same man he was 48 hours ago; it was an impossibility, because he now shared a dark secret with only a handful of other people in the world. Yet he was still required, indeed *expected* to continue as though nothing had changed; that meant keeping secret from everyone everything he had learned over the last couple of days. *Everyone*, including the two people he normally shared things with: Nina, his wife and Jenny, his Secretary of State. That would be the hard part.

The more Gerry thought about it the more daunting it became. He knew from past experience how cunning women could be. He knew that contrary to popular belief women do not really *nag*, they *inquire*. And that was not all, somehow they possessed an uncanny knack of asking the *right* questions. Even when they do not know what they are asking about they still manage to ask the right questions. He believed that women were the world's most patient detectives, invariably uncovering the truth while leaving the man clueless as to exactly how he had been found out. The only thing more tenacious and probing than a wife is a wife with an ally. Whatever one misses, the other is guaranteed to pick up on.

Gerry knew this because over the years he had learned that although he shared his personal secrets with Nina, she could usually also manage to wheedle some of the more important state concerns out of him. Likewise, he only told Jenny of state matters, yet she still tended to find out personal secrets from Nina anyway. He had also learned that where his wife was concerned it tended not to matter what answers he gave: she still came to the right conclusion. He couldn't help but feel that not only did Luc ask a lot from people, but had he spent more time in the company of women he would then know the magnitude of what he asked.

As they reached the gates of the White House, it dawned on him that he had no idea what 'he' had done at Camp David or what had occurred in the *real* world during his absence. He seriously hoped **nothing** had happened or, at least nothing he was expected to do anything about. Hopefully, the front pages were full of an ageing movie star's geriatric birth, latest toy-boy, or similar and not national or global disasters. As it turned out, he was safe but being back would still take some adjusting to.

He spent his first day back in solitude, officially available if necessary but hoping that 'necessary' wouldn't occur. He desperately needed time to pigeonhole his thoughts and emotions before locking them safely away—somewhere Nina and Jenny couldn't get at them.

Also, he needed to investigate the contents of the envelope the stranger had handed him at the airfield.

Inside the envelope was a micro disc showing the last 48 hours at Camp David. Relief swept over him as he watched the disc, taking careful note of exactly what he was supposed to have said and done.

It felt very peculiar watching a stranger be his double and doing it so accurately as well. Technically, 48 hours takes exactly that to watch, but by speeding up things such as sleeping, using the bathroom, or watching TV (unless it was the news), it can be condensed down to a reasonable viewing time. At least now he knew what telephone conversations he'd had with Nina; she would've been bound to catch him out otherwise. He could envisage her coming out with comments that would flummox him, which would undoubtedly arouse her suspicion. Her first line of attack was nearly always the dreaded:

"You know what you said the other night?"

Or the equally horrifying:

"I'm so glad we had that chat yesterday; I never knew you felt like X about Y." The disc was lifesaving.

Gerry returned to work the following day and after the standard welcome back meeting to update him, he tried to settle back into his normal routine. His main priority was the rebuilding of America and her wounded economy. It was not an easy task but one which, to his credit, ran relatively smoothly: it was only slightly over schedule and only exceeded its budget by a couple of billion dollars. This illustrious achievement was not all due to President McQuillan's political leadership and organisational skills. In a world where virtually every country needed aid, there was neither the funding nor the ability to raise funds. Quite simply, had the budget been any further stretched work would have come to a grinding halt anyway.

By the spring of 2049, America was, for better or worse nearly back to her old self apart from the rugged volcanic landscape, which had been changed forever.

2049 also saw the first proper daylight since the eruption—the dusky veil that had covered the globe for years was finally being lifted and for most people that meant a brighter, clearer future was on the way.

There were still a few very vivid sunsets, but these began to occur less frequently throughout the year, not that anybody really cared. People were more than willing to trade spectacular sunsets for proper daylight. The White House too had more or less returned to how it was before the eruption, but the relationships which had been forged during the volcanic winter continued to remain strong. Experiences like that build friendships that last an eternity: friendships like that of Gerry McQuillan and his secretary of state, Jenny Peters.

Despite the fact that she had now moved back home they continued their morning coffee sessions, and she would still tease him about how he read the papers cover to cover.

"Slow down Gerry, you might miss a comma." and "Don't forget to read all the margins."

He didn't mind this, as if nothing else it showed that he had managed to successfully keep Luc and their agenda a secret from her and Nina. Had they had the least suspicion that he was keeping something from them, he felt quite sure that he would've been the subject of a female interrogation. In his opinion being a source of amusement was far safer.

Since the first meeting in 2047, Gerry and the other project members had continued to meet with Luc every six months for updates. By 2049 several changes had taken place: the disused airfield had been re-opened, the roads had got safer, and security around the President had been increased. Every time something changed Gerry wondered how he would get to the next meeting. Luc, however, was both resourceful and inventive, proving to Gerry he was not in the least bit concerned by these changes.

Most buildings where heads of state reside have underground bunkers, passages, or both where the leader in question can either escape unnoticed or take shelter. Camp David is no exception, and Luc probably knew more about what lay beneath it than any president.

To Luc it was a bit of a game, with Gerry not knowing exactly where in the grounds of Camp David he would meet the man he had named 'John'. Gerry chose the name because that was where he used to meet him: in the 'John'. He also discovered that the Ghosts could become just that—Ghosts.

Had Gerry actually given it much thought, he would've put two and two together and realised that Luc had been working with American Presidents since the late 1940s—long before the Yellowstone eruption.

Apart from the actual agenda, Gerry couldn't help but like the time he spent at Luc's house; he suspected it was the same for the rest of the guests. Kabal and his wife Layna were also present at most of these meetings, sharing their plans for the future of humankind on Mars. Layna, it turned out, would have an unenviable role in the new world as she explained on one occasion:

"I have the job of teaching these children to be parents. You must all remember that these children have never belonged to a proper family unit. Despite the fact that they are of superior intelligence and will be aged between 19 and 22 when they leave Earth, they are still very naive in certain matters ... parenthood, relationships, sex, etcetera. Unlike you or I they will not grieve for the Earth, and this is because they have only ever seen the inside of the hidden facilities. They do not know what it is to lie on a sun-drenched beach or what it is like to build a snowman, and these are things they will probably never get to experience. What they *will* experience is the same chaotic sense of freedom a wild animal feels when you open the cage and let it run free for the first time. This is something that will require patience and guidance and *that* ... well, that is where I come in.

Hopefully, my experience with the children from all the facilities will be beneficial. I am also hoping that because my marriage to Kabal is strong, it will serve as an example for them to follow. I'm sure you are all relieved to know that we *do* believe in the sanctity of marriage ..." directing the last comment largely at Pope Gregory, she elaborated further ... "You see, basically two heads are always better than one and in a good marriage where two people work together, great things can be achieved. Without this sort of partnership, the resulting sexual freedom has its own set of hazards: jealousy and disease being the largest and most obvious problems. But there is also the lack of any proper family structure to consider." She could see the questioning looks on their faces.

"I accept that these children did not have what you or I would regard as 'proper families'," she continued, in response to their puzzled expressions, "but that was purely out of necessity. There was no other way to ensure either the safety of these children or the success of their mission. That does not mean that they are laboratory rats who have been just created, trained, and left without any sort of love or attention. They are indeed very real children who were played with when they were younger, cuddled, and tucked up in bed, etcetera. It is just that the mother and father figures were replaced by Luc, Kabal, and me, along with the scientists who taught and cared for them. Anyway, as I was saying before, in an unstable or polygamous society men and women do not form a close enough bond with each other to pool their resources and abilities. This makes them less productive. I think, I may have my work cut out for me, but I will do my best not to let any of you down."

Gerry glanced across at Ghazal, wondering what he had made of the last few comments; he didn't have to wait long to find out.

"Layna ..." began Ghazal.

She looked at the Saudi Prince, aware that she may well have offended him although her look of sincerity showed that she very much hoped that was not the case.

"I just wanted you to know that I think you are right. It is sad, but I do not have the bond with any of my wives that I should have. They have become a mark of wealth in most polygamous societies, not the companions they should be. I think you and Kabal will achieve great things on Mars, and I wish you every success."

Everyone agreed, although it had not really occurred to anyone in the room that they might not be successful. They were obviously as deeply committed to the project as Luc himself was.

Whilst their commitment was never questioned, what *was* questioned was the amount of time these leaders had spent in office.

Kuan Yin was the first to voice his concerns over what he referred to as a 'Genara' Erection'. Aside from the Crown Prince of Saudi and the Pontiff, they all shared Kuan Yin's concerns.

It wasn't that any of them were actually experiencing political unrest within their governments; it was just a concern that it would happen soon. The world was getting back to normal because these leaders had done all the hard work necessary, and they expected challenges from those who believed they would have an easier ride.

"Did I not say at our first meeting that you would be the last leaders I would meet with before the end?" Luc looked despondent by their lack of faith in what he said.

"Why do you now think otherwise? Why did you not question this at the beginning? I would not have said it if it were not true. I suppose that if you insist on having these doubts you will just have to wait and see ... Before you leave, there is something more important I wish to mention: it is the asteroid. I know you are all concerned because none of your astronomers have seen it yet, but that does not make it any the less real. You cannot see love and hate, but you know they exist ... I'm afraid once again you will have to trust me on this, but I should imagine that it is only a matter of time and of course, looking in the right place ... I will elaborate further next time."

Gerry, like everyone else, very much wanted him to be wrong, hoping he was just another eccentric millionaire obsessed by Armageddon. However, despite preferring that option he very much doubted it was likely.

Luc was, of course proved right when in July 2049 they heard the first whispers from astronomers of a catastrophic asteroid. As it turned out, it had been detected several years earlier but until now had been believed to be of no significant threat. Now, however, it had changed direction, and was apparently heading straight for Earth with yet another extinction-level disaster forecast.

Astronomers were, nonetheless, somewhat unclear as to exactly why it had changed course: presumably, this was because they didn't really know. There were plenty of vague theories from some of the more eminent astronomers and astrophysicists, including it being knocked off course by either another meteor or other space debris, the Yarkovsky effect, and of course a lot of blurb about gravity. The bottom line was they had no idea whatsoever but were expected to have an explanation anyway. At the end of the day, it didn't really matter what theories they put forward, none of them altered the fact that it *had* changed course; it was going to hit Earth unless someone came up with a way to stop it. The only thing that was clear was the estimated date of impact: September 28th, 2055.

This didn't come as any surprise to Gerry or the others, but it did provide them with a harsh reminder that not only was Luc right, but that they only had six years of life left.

The majority of people were somewhat naively unconcerned about the asteroid, despite media headlines heralding the end of the world. This was largely due to the fact that they had only recently survived Yellowstone and weren't quite ready for another global disaster just yet.

Governments across the globe were allegedly 'implementing strategies': a meaningless phrase designed to offer reassurance when politicians want to be seen to be doing something useful.

Probably the most useful thing they did was attending the emergency meeting Luc arranged at the first mention of the asteroid. It was here they discovered that the asteroid the media was making such a fuss about was apparently of no threat whatsoever to Earth.

"It will pass very close, I grant you." Luc explained at the meeting. "There may also be several unpleasant environmental effects: volcanic activity, earthquakes, tsunamis, etcetera."

"Nothing new then," groaned the Aussie P.M.

"Okay. Let me just get this straight ..." All eyes, especially Luc's, were now focused on Gerry.

"... We're gonna get hit by an asteroid in 2055 ... but not the same asteroid the astronomers say is gonna hit us ... a different one. Right?"

Luc nodded.

"So, just for the record ... exactly how many asteroids are there hanging around space with our name on them?"

"Well Gerry ..." smiled Luc, "... and just for the record ... it must be ..." Luc smacked his lips together, and shook his head before adding, "... thousands probably ... if not millions."

It was all very gallows humour, but he got a smile out of everyone at what was proving to be a very solemn discussion.

"Unfortunately," Luc continued, his tone of voice bringing the mood back to a more serious level. "Unlike most of them, the one with our name on that will destroy us isn't as far away as the others. I am afraid that even if it *was* detected by your astronomers you wouldn't be able to do anything to stop it. I am sorry."

His tone changed at the end of the sentence, from that of a schoolteacher to just plain sorrow. It was clear to all that

Luc had no doubt whatsoever that what he was saying was the absolute truth, but none of it stopped the brief, somewhat sceptical inquisition that followed.

"Once again I am surrounded by 'Doubting Thomases' ... just because your astronomers have seen a large asteroid that must obviously be *'The One'*. I agree that if this one *did* hit Earth it would have disastrous consequences for most, if not all of us, but it *won't* and the one that *will* hit us is much larger, denser, and far more ... well ... *dangerous*. The reason your people have not seen it is because it will come from interstellar space, which means it will probably not be picked up by your observatories until a week or so before impact. There are a couple of reasons for this: firstly, they appear dim in interstellar space, making them very difficult to see; secondly, by the time they are close enough to be detected, they are easily camouflaged by the stars around them. Also, this particular asteroid is on a direct collision course with earth, so although it is very large there is not much movement across the sky. In a nutshell, you would be very lucky to see it."

"But *you* have seen it ... *Haven't you, Luc*?" Ella's line of questioning was half-rhetorical, as she only assumed he had probably seen it. What she didn't know, was *how*.

"Yes, Ella, I have seen it." He hesitated slightly ...

"... but even if you did see it what do you think you would be able to do? It is 53 kilometres in diameter—it will wipe us out in less than a day—probably within minutes. Very quickly and very violently. Even if you manage to break it up, each fragment would be big enough to cause an extinction-level cataclysm, and there would be rather a lot of fragments. For those of you who remain sceptical, and should you really desire to see it I can show it to you, but I fail to see how it will make you feel any better. However, if you wish to see the cause of your own demise please come with me."

Luc showed them to his observatory, which was not a room with a few computers and monitors as they had expected. This room was a hexagonal shape with each of the six walls being made of glass and a different view out of each. The rest of the room had the usual deep white carpet and soft white leather seating. The only difference was a computer terminal built into an arm of each sofa.

It turned out that the walls were not just windows: they were, in fact, huge computer screens linked to the terminals. None of Luc's house guests knew much about astronomy, but they did know that this was far superior to any observatory they had ever set foot in. The images on the screens were so crystal clear it seemed as though the house was, itself, floating in outer space and if anyone opened the window they would be able to literally touch the stars. It was also very apparent that the high-resolution images on the screens came from far beyond the solar system.

"Here ... here is your executioner." Luc was pointing to one of the screens, which showed a large spherical object spinning through space.

"I expected it to be more ... well ... irregular in shape ... I mean ... I don't know too much about this sort of thing ..." Ella's voice tailed off as she ran out of things to mumble about.

"It's ok Ella, you are absolutely right. It *is* a somewhat unusual asteroid: normally you would expect spherical asteroids to be much larger with diameters of 150 kilometres upwards. This one, although only 53 kilometres appears to have enough self-gravitation to either form or maintain a spherical shape."

"Wh ... what is it made of?" stammered the Russian, appearing quite shaken by the asteroid.

"Well ... normally they would be made up of a mixture of iron, ice, and/or carbon, but this one is made of a much denser metal mixed with carbon and water traces."

Had it not been heading straight towards Earth, they could've viewed it as the beautiful, wondrous, heavenly body it was. Instead, it was an object of fear and hatred, a U.F.O.—Unwanted Flying Object.

"Can't you ... vaporise it or something? I mean, you have far better technology than us. Surely you can deflect it, destroy it, or do something with it!"

Although Gerry had asked the question the rest of them all nodded and murmured their support. Luc looked despondent; he had expected that question sooner or later.

"If I *could*, don't you think I *would*? Unfortunately, it is not that simple. Yes, my technology is superior to yours and maybe, given another scenario I could help, but regrettably not this time ... it isn't a normal asteroid. You can see that by its shape and the speed it is travelling. Look, I'm truly sorry, but I am doing all that I can. Saving enough of the human race to ensure its continuation as a species is all I can do. I am *sorry* it isn't *more.*"

There was a slight hint of sarcasm in his voice, which he felt they deserved because they appeared to be forgetting that without him the human race would have faced certain extinction. He alone had achieved far more than they could even contemplate doing, yet instead of any thanks for what he had done they were just complaining about what he couldn't or wouldn't do. He never offered any further explanation as to why he was unable to destroy it; they just had to accept the fact that he couldn't.

It wasn't until they were making their way to the lift for their journey home that Luc added any further comment:

"I feel that now would be a very good time to take stock of not only your own lives, but also the people close to you. Till next time, my friends." That was all Luc said before the lift doors closed and they went back to their lives.

Once back home their lives consisted of endless U.N. meetings to discuss the best course of preventative action to take. This meant trying to reach a unanimous decision as to whether they should attempt to destroy the asteroid their astronomers *had* discovered, using either chemical or nuclear weapons or try to deflect it using ion propulsion. The downside of nudging it out of the way using an ion drive craft was firstly, it would still require a conventional rocket to launch it out of the Earth's atmosphere and secondly, it would be very expensive. Most countries were still struggling to revive their economies. There was also the question as to who would build one. N.A.S.A.'s jet propulsion lab had been destroyed in the mega-quake that had occurred during the Yellowstone eruption along with several of their other U.S. space research centres. There were still operational sites dotted around the world, although in fairness these were much smaller outfits most of which had only really been used to launch satellites and none of which had been in use since Yellowstone.

As for destroying the asteroid using nuclear weapons, that had drawbacks too. There *were* stockpiles of weapons available, and whilst launching them *probably* wouldn't be too much of a problem the fragments of rock caused by this method might well be a bigger problem than the asteroid. Even though this asteroid, according to Luc, was of no threat it was still 10 miles in diameter and a single fragment had the potential to be devastating. Besides which, the rest of the world knew nothing of Luc, his fantastic observatory, or the *real* 'Doomsday Asteroid'.

In the end it was a different option altogether that was decided to be the safest and of course, most cost-effective strategy. This would involve attempting to nudge it off course, so to speak, using strategically aimed nuclear weapons. The overall plan involved using a nuclear missile as opposed to using an unmanned, *suicide* spacecraft to push the asteroid off course. This would've been far too expensive in a poverty-stricken world, whereas using any remaining nuclear weapons was a far cheaper option. Most of the remaining weapons would be needed due to the sheer size of the asteroid and there was, of course still the risk of damaging the asteroid causing fragments to hit the Earth anyway.

They were damned if they did, and damned if they didn't. Or so it seemed.

Within days of the U.N. reaching the decision to 'nuke 'n' nudge', more news came in from some of the observatories: news claiming that the asteroid may well get very close but, in their opinion, would not actually collide with Earth. This news came from many of the same astronomers, who up until now had claimed the asteroid was on a definite collision course with

Earth. This allowed the people of America to maintain their naive indifference to the matter; they just weren't ready for anything else to happen to them despite the panic-mongering media coverage that gradually became more fervent with each new development. To the media, astronomers had now replaced rock-stars and royalty.

It appeared that the rift the asteroid caused within the astronomical community was nothing short of a reporter's wet dream come true. Every single broadsheet, tabloid, magazine, and scandal-rag had 'Hit or Miss' headlines of some description. This gave Gerry and the others a chance to persuade the U.N. to hold fire, at least until there was agreement as to exactly where this asteroid was headed.

It would be two very long years before it became evident that this asteroid was of no threat: July 6th, 2131.

A wave of relief swept over the world, adorned with a certain smugness that once again the human race had prevailed.

Unfortunately for the select few, it was becoming more and more likely that Luc was right. This meant that while the rest of the world were busy preferring the headlines that suggested the whole thing was probably a false alarm, Gerry and the other project members knew the truth. To them, this was just a practice run.

The White House was no exception; it too was caught up in the euphoria that swarmed the globe that day. Gerry desperately wanted to share that feeling, but he just couldn't. The relief was so overwhelming that nobody, not even Nina and Jenny noticed Gerry's feeble attempt at 'faking it'.

However, once alone, the public face withered as he thought about the truth. How ignorant and stupid people could be: always wanting to know the truth as if it was something wondrously enlightening. The Holy Grail of knowledge: parents demand it of their children, lovers are obsessed by it, scientists, philosophers, and theologians spend lifetimes looking for it. Well, he knew the truth and it wasn't wondrous; it was black and ominous, and he hated it. Even if he could've shared it with someone, he probably wouldn't. Why share such misery with others?

As far as Gerry McQuillan was concerned, the harsh black truth was that he had survived the worst natural disaster in history: he lived through a dark, cold, volcanic winter. He had nursed a devastated country and economy back to health, only to see it all destroyed a few years later by nothing more than a lump of rock. That was his truth and knowing it, he decided to take Luc's advice and make the most of what time there was left.

CHAPTER 11

Gerry looked at the faces seated around the large oval table: a mixture of wide-eyed anticipation and confusion looked back at him. He took a deep breath and slowly began his speech:

"It has not escaped my notice, although I seriously doubt it was supposed to, that there is a growing political unrest within this office."

He took another deep breath before continuing:

"... Nor has it escaped my notice that this has only started over the last couple of years ... in fact only since the asteroid threat passed. Quite a coincidence, wouldn't you say?"

There were a few sheepish expressions, but Gerry wasn't giving anyone the opportunity to comment before continuing:

"It seems somewhat odd wouldn't you say? How no one ... not even the extremely ambitious Ashley Jeferis ..."

Ashley went to speak, but Gerry wasn't ready to give him the chance just yet.

"Oh, don't look so wounded Ashley ... it was your ambition to take over the world that made you such a good vice president in the first place. But is it not true to say Ashley that from the start of the Yellowstone disaster until the announcement that there was no asteroid threat to Earth absolutely no one, not even you, has even considered holding an election? However, now that the world is the calmest it's ever been ... now it seems that everyone wants to be President. Well, for the record, I agree. I think we should have an election."

He paused briefly to take yet another deep breath.

"It's a New World and therefore it deserves new rules ... a new constitution ... or at least an amended one." He paused, this time to hear any comments. There were none, so he continued.

"I propose that each citizen's vote should count as we now have a much-reduced population. I don't know about you, but I think the old college system could end up being a bit of a farce; like I said before, it is a *new* world, and *everybody* should have a say who's in Government. I also think the length of office should be increased to five years: four years doesn't give anyone much time to make a difference."

"Not eleven years then?" muttered a very disconcerted vice president.

"If you like Ashley, but I'd make it easier than the last eleven if I was you."

"Humph," added Ashley feebly.

"Where was I? … Oh yes, new rules. I suppose that decreasing the age restriction to thirty wouldn't hurt and I believe that there should be no limit on the number of times someone can be President; after all, you will only be voted in if the general public think you're any good. And before anyone thinks this is purely to allow my *own* re-election, I don't plan on doing any campaigning. I just want a quiet retirement. So, are there any questions? … *Or comments?"* His eyes fixed in Ashley's direction, which didn't go unnoticed by Ashley. He thought for a moment before asking:

"So, do they still have to be American citizens? 'Cos I expect there's some illegal Mexican immigrants who might like to run."

"Oh, very amusing I'm sure, Ashley … but in case you hadn't noticed we do not actually have the population we used to have, and we don't have quite so many people over thirty-five anymore; at least, not fit, and healthy ones. In fact, by the time you narrow it down to the number of healthy over thirty-fives who want to run for President I imagine we'd be left with Ashley here. And of course, a couple of

Mexican immigrants looking for work permits. Quite honestly, I don't really think we have much choice but to make changes, do you? We shall however take a vote on these proposals and any others that are put forward and for the record, yes, I do think that candidates should be U.S. citizens."

"What about the Senate? Should their rules be amended as well?"

"I don't think so, Jenny." Ashley hastened to get his ten cents worth in.

"It was already amended to allow 21-year-olds to run for Senate a few years ago; if we amend it again we'll end up with a bunch of juveniles running the country."

"*Thank you, Ashley* ... for your insight. You are, however, quite right; I think that 21 is quite low enough."

Eventually, after what turned out to be a very arduous meeting the amendments Gerry had proposed were agreed upon. The date for elections would, however, remain the same: the Tuesday following the first Monday in November. Now though, it would be every five years instead of every four and candidates were now required to have been resident in the U.S. for a decade instead of 14 years. This, however, could prove challenging to verify as a vast amount of state records were missing since the eruption.

As for Gerry, he was happily looking forward to retirement, or so he kept telling everyone. He thought that *maybe … just maybe …* if he convinced enough people how great retirement would be then somewhere along the line he might just convince himself. It's doubtful that anyone was truly convinced by this, and he certainly wasn't fooling his wife.

The new election rules were to be announced on the 15th of August 2053; the date was also Gerry's 60th birthday, thus allowing him to announce his retirement at the same time.

Over the last few years, he had given a lot of thought to Luc's comment about how they would be the last world leaders he would have any dealings with. Initially he had thought this was impossible, but several years later it had stopped being quite so unrealistic. It had only been in the last couple of years that the numbers meeting at Luc's house had begun to dwindle. He now knew that Luc wasn't bothering with their successors, presumably because everything was now in place for the children's evacuation to Mars. He also knew that those who did not attend the meetings were blissfully unaware of the project, and more to the point—the asteroid.

Gerry considered that to be the only attractive part of retirement: no knowledge of what was to come until it was too late to worry about it. The downside was the prospect of having his memory erased and of course, the boredom. He had always enjoyed the adventure involved in attending one of Luc's meetings; there was an action-hero feel about them and the thought of not being part of that anymore was bad enough, but not even having his memories of it was worse.

Still, he had made his decision and he would have to live with it. After all, even if he ran for President there were no guarantees that he'd be elected again.

✷

The morning of Gerry McQuillan's 60th birthday began with sunlight streaming in through the open curtains; he could feel the warmth on his face. He stretched and lay back, enjoying the cosy feel of the morning sun. Daylight was something he was sure he would *never* take for granted again.

Half asleep, he reached across the bed, but it was empty. Nina must be cooking breakfast he thought, hoping it would be a 'Full English'. This was one of the pleasures he had enjoyed before he came to office: long weekends that began with Nina cooking him a 'Full English' breakfast. *That* was his idea of 'Quality Time'.

The day after it was announced that the asteroid was of no threat to Earth whatsoever, Nina had got up early and cooked Gerry his favourite breakfast. He had enjoyed it so much that it had become a daily occurrence: every morning Nina got up and made breakfast. What she made varied, but it was always good to sit down together; to Gerry, it came under the heading of 'making the most of the time we have left'.

The relaxed feel of the morning sun made the current political situation seem very insignificant. After forcing himself out of bed and into the routine of showering and dressing, he made his way to the kitchen. As he approached, he took a deep breath instantly recognising the mouth-watering aroma that could only be bacon.

"Mmm, Full English. Happy birthday to me." He grinned, putting his arms around his wife.

"Happy birthday, Gerry." She kissed him and smiled.

"I think I like being 60 ... it's pretty good so far ... sunshine, my favourite breakfast, *and* a kiss ..."

"Go and sit down. I'll bring your breakfast over to you." On the table was a present.

"Can I open this?"

"No! You can't. Wait 'til I sit down ... Don't be so impatient."

Gerry groaned,

"Aw ... go on ..."

Gerry adopted this childlike behaviour whenever Nina bought him something; it was a form of compensation for Nina not having any of her own children to spoil.

Within seconds of finishing his sentence Nina groaned and began to fall. He leapt up out of his seat, managing to catch her before she hit the floor. She was clutching her chest and gasping for air.

"Oh God ... No ... Nina ... talk to me ... talk to me, Nina." Frantically Gerry reached into his pocket for his cell phone, still desperately holding on to his wife.

"Oh, please answer ... hurry up ... Oh, thank God. Hello ... um ... yes ... it's President McQuillan ... it's my wife ... she's having a heart attack ... or ... or ... I don't know ... she can't breathe ... please just hurry."

He clicked the phone down. He wasn't calm or reassuring; had it been anybody else lying on the kitchen floor he might have been, but he could see that Nina was losing her fight.

She tried to speak but the words wouldn't come out; eventually, and despite all his shushing attempts, she mustered up enough breath to whisper very faintly:

"Win for me."

Then she was still.

He screamed, not really anything comprehensible, just a pained scream. He held her tightly in his arms as the tears rolled down his face and dripped quietly onto her lifeless body.

The paramedics arrived and tried to coax Gerry into letting go of his wife, but the more they coaxed the closer he held her.

It wasn't until Jenny Peters' arrival on the scene that Gerry finally released Nina into the paramedics' charge and even then it took Jenny a while to convince him to let her go.

She sat him down and proceeded to call the White House doctor; she felt sure that Gerry must be in shock, he certainly looked unable to cope with anything much. The election announcements would just have to be made by Vice President Ashley Jeferis who would be all too willing to oblige.

The death of the First Lady, a Presidential election, and the President's forthcoming retirement from office was enough to keep the media circus that followed busy for weeks. Gerry didn't take much notice of it all, right now he had a funeral to arrange and a lot more grieving to do. The funeral was *actually* arranged largely by Jenny, trying to convince Gerry exactly what *Nina* would've wanted. This was not the easiest task as Gerry was suffering from the inevitable blank-mindedness that accompanies grief.

Jenny would ask a question … Gerry would fail to answer … Jenny would make an educated suggestion … Gerry would either agree or disagree. In the event of him disagreeing, she would keep making suggestions until he agreed.

The funeral was very small and discreet, as State funerals go; Gerry did not want all the pomp and ceremony of such an occasion. Now that he'd had time to think about it he had come to the conclusion that assuming Luc was right about the asteroid, Nina may well be better off. Besides which, once he had got over the initial shock of losing his wife he kept telling himself the funeral was nothing more than the burial of a box with a body in it. It wasn't Nina. She would always be alive in his memory. It didn't seem to matter though as none of it made the funeral any easier to cope with on the day.

As the coffin was lowered into the ground Gerry looked around at the people who had attended. Through his tears he caught sight of a man in the distance; he thought the man resembled Luc, but he was too far away and too blurry for Gerry to see that clearly. He thought it would be very unlikely that Luc would attend the funeral as he had never met Nina, but he did kind of like the idea that Luc might be there out of respect for him.

It was at that point that he remembered how clearly Luc had described the asteroid impact as resulting in a quick, but violent death. He did not wish that on his wife. He did not wish a heart attack on his wife either, but he hoped that maybe she had suffered the lesser of the two evils.

Needless to say, friends and colleagues went to great lengths to explain to him how 'time is a great healer'. Every time he heard this he wasn't entirely sure whether to laugh or cry. How much time exactly does it take to heal that amount of pain? He presumed it would take a lot longer than the two years that were left.

It wasn't until after the funeral, when Gerry was alone that he finally opened the birthday present from Nina. As he did so he remembered how perfectly that day had started, and how

devastatingly it had ended. The present that had taken him so long to open was a gold watch: a watch her great-grandfather had been given on his retirement. On the back were the words:
'Win for me'.
   The card that went with it read:

'Retirement is for old men.
   Win for me, President McQuillan.
      Love Always.
         Nina.'

He sat staring at the words, trying to take them in. He remembered that it was the last thing she had said, and now she was saying it again. He loved his wife very much and would normally have done anything she asked, but this was different. He wasn't sure he was up to campaigning. Not now. He was very tired. After all, it had been a very long and difficult few years, with the last week being the most traumatic of all.
   At the same time, he wasn't entirely sure he wanted to retire just yet either. Retirement didn't have quite the same appeal now Nina was no longer there to share it with him.
   He returned to work the day after the funeral. He had the feeling that if he stayed home any longer he may well drive himself

mad. He considered that too much grieving is probably as unhealthy as not grieving at all. Furthermore, he felt quite sure that come 2055, wherever Nina might be she was most likely far better off there than she would be here.

He stared at the photograph on his desk: their wedding photograph. He allowed his mind to wander back to their early years together. All the special times they had shared and how beautiful she had looked. He smiled as he remembered how her mother had said he was a daydreamer, and how he would never amount to anything. He so wished she had stayed alive long enough to see him become President.

He remembered the man who looked like Luc at the funeral, and the meetings at Luc's house. He smiled at the photo on the desk.

"I'll never forget you … In fact, I'll never forget *anything.*"

He reached for the phone,

"Jen, I'm going to run for President … What d'ya think?"

"Thank God, Gerry, I was beginning to think you might be serious about retiring."

"Nah. Not yet."

"Let's get campaigning then … *Mr President.*"

He leant back in his chair. That felt good—he would rather face the asteroid than lose any of his memories.

He winked at the photo,

"I'm gonna win for ya, Nina; you wait and see."

CHAPTER 12

Dear Gerry,

    I am writing to inform you of my impending resignation as once again, President McQuillan, you have proved to be a formidable opponent. Nothing would please me more than to be able to say luck was on your side, but no one could reasonably consider the last twelve years to be 'lucky'. Your ability to preside over a country in times of crisis is admirable, to say the least.
    However, I feel that I have come second for long enough and have therefore decided that as I am never, as you put it 'going to rule the world', now would seem to be as good a time as any to resign from office and lick my wounds in a less public setting.
    I am genuinely proud to have worked alongside you and if I wasn't quite so ambitious, I would have been more than happy to continue as your vice president. Unfortunately, I **am** ambitious and have always hoped that I would become President one day but recently it has become evident that this will never happen.

I am quite sure that I must sound like a sulking child. That is probably because I am.

Sulking and resentment are not good qualities for anyone, let alone a politician and most certainly not for the vice president of such an important country. I wish I felt differently and could continue working alongside you, but sadly this is not the case.

My official resignation has been tendered through the appropriate channels. I just felt that after years of having you not only as a work colleague but also a friend, I owed you a more personal and less formal explanation.

I wish you every success for the future. Who knows? Next time I might even vote for you myself.

Yours sincerely,

Ashley Jefris

Ashley had initially built his campaign on continuing Gerry McQuillan's 'Good work'. This was a plan that had gone horribly wrong the minute Gerry had announced that he was running for President after all. Therefore, this letter did not come as any real surprise to Gerry, who was fully aware that Ashley would have been more than disappointed at not being elected President. None of this altered the fact that he would be sorry to lose him as vice president, even more so as he didn't much like the man who would be replacing him. A certain Kyle Samuels who, in Gerry's opinion was far too loud and overbearing for his own good. Not to mention the fact that he knew nothing about being a politician; after all, what could he possibly know about being vice president? He was only a car salesman from New Jersey.

It had obviously escaped Gerry's notice that over the last two hundred years several people had not only run for office but been elected President and most of them were far less likely to know anything about running a country than Kyle Samuels. At least he knew how to run his own business.

It was doubtful that Kyle Samuels had ever really expected to get into power, particularly as he had amassed a lot less votes than either Gerry or Ashley Jefris; between the two of them, they had pretty much ruled the campaign. Circumstances however, meant this man would be vice president whether Gerry liked him or not.

For Gerry, being re-elected had come more as a relief than a triumph—he hadn't let Nina down and he would be able to keep his memory of Luc. Apart from the obvious fear of what the memory erasing process might entail, he had actually come to view Luc as a friend. A very clever, somewhat eccentric friend but a friend nonetheless, and one with impeccable timing as the familiar advert that appeared in the Washington Post a few days later couldn't have come at a better time for Gerry. What with all the upheaval of Ashley resigning, Kyle being sworn in, and, of course his wife's death, he was just about in need of a holiday and a trip to Luc's surreal world seemed just the thing—particularly as Luc had left it far longer than usual to get in touch and Gerry was beginning to think he may *never* see him again.

  He went to Camp David the night before the meeting with Luc but unlike the first occasion he genuinely wanted time alone to think. So much had happened over the last few years it would be asking a lot for *any* man to cope with it all. Gerry had faced up to and coped with all the traumas and considering it was all on top of trying to run the most powerful country in the world, it was no mean achievement.

  Subsequently, he spent a very restless night at Camp David with his brain activity refusing to give in and let his body have the rest it so desperately needed. This was going to be the first meeting with Luc and the others since the death of his wife. It had been a long and very stressful time since the last meeting. It was different now: he no longer needed to worry so much about what he had done at home whilst away because nobody would be so interested anymore and although he missed Nina, there was a certain convenience to her not being present at the moment. This time he could focus on remembering and enjoying every aspect of the journey or at least the bits during which he would be conscious.

He firmly believed that he had come so close to losing these memories that it was important not to take them for granted; he also felt sure that those others who were still present at the meetings must feel the same way. After all, he wanted all his memories to stay fresh in his mind forever, therefore the others *must* feel the same way. Unfortunately, he also remembered that forever wasn't such a long time anymore. In fact, there was now only about 21 months before the asteroid would turn *forever* into *eternity*.

As always, Gerry had no idea where he would run into John but was fortunately awake enough to see him through the shower cubicle, thereby reducing some of the shock of finding a stranger in his shower. The two men smiled at each other; it was hard to tell whether John was amused by the situation or just by Gerry's reaction to it.

With no security guards or bugs nearby, Gerry spoke to John for the first time.

"I wish I knew more about you ... I mean, I don't even know your *real* name."

"It is best that you and everyone else know me as Gerry McQuillan, besides which, you don't need to know anything about me. It is only important that I know everything about you ..."

Gerry didn't have time to think of anything else to say before a Ghost appeared outside the shower cubicle too.

"Now, if you don't mind I'm trying to have a shower ..."

Gerry left the shower grinning at the only bit of evidence that showed John did have a sense of humour and more importantly, a personality.

Inside Luc's stealth craft he noticed how the number of guests had diminished. He felt an overwhelming sadness at their absence, assuming that they no longer knew of Luc or the curious world they had been part of; not that he had much time to give it any thought before the pleasing aroma that filled the craft sent him into a deep state of unconsciousness.

The Ghost woke him as always. He loved the sound of their voices:

"Mmmm ... I am so glad I will remember this," he yawned.

"What do you mean? Why wouldn't you?"

"Oh ... mm ... yes." He was slightly more awake now and could tell the Ghost was trying to make sense of his sleepy mumbles.

"Well ... had I lost the election then my memory would've been erased ... Right?"

"Yes."

"Well then ... I wouldn't remember any of this, which would be a shame. I wouldn't like that ... you see?"

"Oh Gerry," sang the Ghost, "You are so funny. How could you be upset by losing a memory you would never have had?"

"Well, I ... I ..."

"Come on Gerry. It's time to see Luc."

Gerry was a little put out by what had really started out as a compliment had somehow ended up with him being made fun of, but he had to concede the Ghost was probably right. *Had* his memory been erased, he would *never have known the memory had been there in the first place.*
He was also right about the number of guests present. He, like the others, was fully aware that neither the Egyptian nor

the Greek would be present. He, like them, had attended President Akil Pasha's funeral a few months prior to this meeting. It was also common knowledge that the Greek, Arubel Christakis, had suffered a very debilitating stroke only a week ago and was not expected to recover.

    Gerry had naively hoped that the others who had lost elections might still attend Luc's house, reasoning that with it being so close to the end Luc may not feel the need to erase memories. Judging by the empty seats he obviously wasn't bothering with their successors. It was becoming clear that when Luc had said they would all be the last Premiers he dealt with, that it did not necessarily mean he would be dealing with them right up until the end. He wondered if Luc had been sufficiently compassionate not to tamper with their memories of him and the project. As far as Gerry was concerned, the memory erasing thing was Luc's only unpleasant trait.

    Seated around what now seemed a very over-sized table were the remaining five of them: Ella James and Steve Cooper, whose countries were holding their elections later in the year; the re-elected Gerry McQuillan, whose place at Luc's table was now quite secure; Pope Gregory

XVIII; and Ghazal, the Crown Prince of Saudi.

"Before I discuss more important matters there are a few things I would like to say ... Firstly, I would like to say how sorry I am that there are not more of you here ... "

"*Luuuc*," interrupted Ella, in her most enquiring tone. Luc fixed his eyes on Ella, gesturing for her to continue: "*Well*, I was just wondering ... the others ... you know ... the ones that aren't here ... well ... did you? ... Well ... you know ..."

"Did I what?" said Luc, his tone of voice showed that he was playing with her.

"You know ... the memory thing." She began to wince as she neared the end of her sentence.

"Oh, *That* ... Yeah, of course. I always do." Ella was starting to look very uncomfortable, yet it was obvious to the rest of them that Luc was being deliberately casual about the whole thing. Realising that Ella wasn't seeing the funny side of her neurosis, Luc set about trying to reassure her instead; she quite obviously wasn't in the mood for Luc's sense of humour.

"I'm sorry, Ella. I didn't mean to scare you. Honestly though, they don't feel anything. No, even better than that: they don't know anything about it ... not even at the time. And I promise you it doesn't erase any other memories, just the ones of either me or the project. It's perfectly safe and harmless. Now does anybody else have anything they want to add before we get back to more important matters?"

"Yeah, I do." grinned the Aussie P.M. "Does the last one get the keys to a space-age chocolate factory?"

"Sorry Steve?" For once, Luc looked slightly baffled.

"Y'know ... it's a children's book. The kids are dwindled down till only one is left ... Charlie ... and he inherits the chocolate factory."

"Yes, thank you. I knew what it was; I'd just ... never really thought of myself as being like Willy Wonka. Anyway, as I was saying before I was turned into a fictional children's character ... I *am* sorry there are not more of you left even if I don't have a chocolate factory to give away ... and yes, I did erase memories ... and no, they didn't feel it." He grinned across at the Australian.

"And no, it didn't involve Oompa-Loompas or chocolate! Still, I am pleased to see all of you that are here."

The Australian, right from their very first meeting had always been the larger-than-life class comedian, either playing the fool or entering into a playful banter with someone. That someone was usually Ella: she would play the outraged feminist to his macho man with Oscar-winning brilliance. This was an intriguing phenomenon, as within the political arena they were both as efficient, and professional as the next stuffed shirt. They kept this behaviour, like everything else that concerned Luc, a closely guarded secret. Now however, they were both looking very sombre indeed.

"Luc … I know you're keen to move on with the meeting … but … well … I … you do know, don't you? That we … that is … Ella and I … have general elections coming up …"

Luc nodded quietly, as Steve continued,

"Well, just in case … you know … I lose … and … well … my memory is erased … I just wanted you all to know it's been … well … an honour …Yes, that's it … an honour being part of this project and a real honour to have known you, Luc. Even if I might not know who you are this time next year; if you know what I mean."

"It's been a pleasure knowing you too. More than that, it's been fun!"

"I don't want my memory erased Luc … Really I don't." Just *saying* the word 'erased' seemed to make her wince.

"*Okay, Ella.*"

Luc rolled his eyes; all he wanted to do was get on with more important matters.

"Will you feel better if I say I won't erase your memory?"

"Well … Yes … I suppose so."

"Right, that's *that* settled. Can we get back to business now? Right, good. In that case, the other thing I am determined to do before there are any more interruptions is to offer my condolences to Gerry on the loss of his wife."

Gerry felt a bit uncomfortable yet at the same time quite privileged that Luc had bothered to mention something so personal. As Luc continued directing his comments to Gerry, he began to wonder whether Luc might have been the man he saw at Nina's funeral or whether he was just getting carried away with his own self-importance. (Egomania can be a common problem among Presidents and Prime Ministers. It is less apparent in royalty but appears to progress rapidly into a severe sociopathic disorder amongst dictators.)

"Also, I am very glad you are here at what I know has been a very difficult time for you."

A slightly red Gerry smiled weakly back but Luc didn't notice; he was on a roll. He fully intended to continue speaking for as long as he could before the next wave of interruptions.

"Finally, before I get down to more important matters I just thought I'd better mention that Kabal and Layna won't be joining us this time as they are busy with the leaving preparations."

That last sentence really hit home to all of them; a harsh reminder of how little time there was left and perhaps in many cases, how that time should be spent. Whilst they were all quietly soul-searching, Luc seized the opportunity to continue uninterrupted.

"Okay, here's the important stuff: you know that there are several ships leaving, carrying food supplies, building materials, medical equipment, etcetera. Well, obviously these supplies won't last forever so we are also sending seeds, bulbs, etcetera, which will be a start. But in order to have a fully functioning ecosystem animals are necessary. Obviously it would be impractical to take herds of cattle and various other forms of wildlife through space, so we decided the most practical solution would be to transport their DNA instead. It takes far less space and is much cleaner and quieter. Plus, the planet will not be completely terraformed when they arrive so this means the DNA can be stored until it is needed, and then … Hey, Presto!

Incidentally, we called this ship 'Noah's Ark'—it seemed appropriate."

"It sounds rather like playing God; I'm not sure I like it much."

"I really would not expect that a deeply spiritual individual such as yourself would like it, but from where I'm sitting our planet and our species is teetering right on the edge of extinction. That is, unless we do something about it. Now ... if you have a better idea or a way of transporting all the animals or, at the very least, a breeding pair from every species on Earth ... one that doesn't involve building a wooden ark and relying on God to help you, which is doable within the next ..."

Luc paused for a moment. He had deliberately avoided telling them what date or even what month the asteroid would hit. He could see the look of anticipation on their faces.

"...X months." He smiled, as he watched their expressions change.

"As I said in the beginning, I will tell you the date at the next meeting."

He was looking at the Pope, to see if he had any further comments to add. Luc didn't for one moment believe that a Pope had ever lived who was above playing God, and that his comment earlier was little more than a token gesture. Just enough humility to secure his seat in heaven. The

Pope's reluctance to add any further comment just served to enhance Luc's opinion.

"Okay. Let's continue ... I shall apologise before I start if I tread on any religious toes, but I am afraid we no longer live in biblical times. For argument's sake, should God appear to save us at the eleventh hour I will be the first in line for Holy Communion at the Vatican. We will have colonised Mars by then, the Earth and inhabitants are all still intact, therefore this next problem will never occur but working on the premise that it doesn't happen that way ... well, here's where you come in. On the off chance that something goes wrong and the human race, despite our efforts, starts to die out ... I seriously hope this will not be the case but just as an emergency measure we have collected DNA samples from all the children, and they are aware of the necessity to do the same with future generations. This is purely an emergency measure ... natural childbirth is ultimately preferable."

"Emergency sperm ... Mmm ... I like that idea ... they could have one of those little glass boxes on the wall. You know, the ones with hammers next to them and signs above them that read: 'In case of extinction. Break glass'"

Steve Cooper had obviously cheered up a bit, bringing Ella back up with him.

She felt better after Luc had said he wouldn't erase her memory; at least, that's what she *thought* he'd said.

"Presumably it would be one of your *many* donations ... eh, Steve?"

"What can I say? Give generously: that's my motto."

Ella groaned; he was beyond all hope.

"That's very thoughtful of you Steve, thank you." Luc was grinning. It was nice to have Steve and Ella back on form and even a much put-out pontiff had been forced to smile.

"And as it turns out, Steve is actually not too far off the mark so before you all look too horrified I'd better explain." Now he had their full attention.

"Without the co-operation of all of you this project would not have been possible. I also added that this is purely an emergency matter. So, let me get to the point. We have collected DNA samples from several people over the years: people who have qualities or traits that would be beneficial to civilisation. This is where you all come in—I would like to take a sample from each of you as you all proved yourselves to be first-class leaders during the harsh years that followed the

Yellowstone disaster, and you also have compassion and a willingness to listen ... and more importantly a willingness to learn. These characteristics are highly admirable ones because if people don't listen then they definitely won't learn. There is more though: not only do I require a DNA sample from each of you, but I would like to collect a sample from a member of the opposite sex. That person is to be of your choosing, not mine."

"How are we supposed to do that? You can't just go up to someone and cut their fingernails or pull their hair."

"No Gerry, you can't ... Well, not unless you don't mind getting slapped. If you give me the name of the person I will collect the sample, okay?"

"How?" enquired Ella, a bit concerned that she would have to nominate a man as she was the only female.

"Don't worry, I'm not going to kill anyone."

"No, I didn't mean that. You're talking about collecting ... well ... you know." She was making her wincing face and looking very embarrassed.

"Ohhh ... I see. Well, I don't think we need to go that far ... Unless of course anyone wants to ..." he redirected his gaze toward the Aussie, who was grinning back.

"All I need to collect is a DNA sample like Gerry said: hair, fingernails, skin, etcetera."

"Oh, that's a relief," smiled Ella sheepishly.

"Are you OK with that? Ghazal? ... Richard?"

Ghazal nodded; he'd been very quiet during this meeting, although that wasn't anything that new. Ghazal was always far more of a listener than a talker, and why interrupt the Steve and Ella floor show?

"I'm fine with it. Honestly, Luc."

"Well, I suppose if everyone else is all right with it I have no choice. I'm not especially comfortable with it, but I'm not going to get into another religious squabble with you either."

"Good. Besides, I'm sure your God will forgive you." He smiled at his guests. It was a warm safe smile, like that of a loving parent.

"I'm afraid it is time to go. I know this meeting has been shorter than usual, but next time I promise we will have more time together."

Luc continued to talk with them as they made their way back to the lift, nothing of any relevance, just small talk. Eventually the lift doors closed. They returned to their lives and Luc to his.

CHAPTER 13

For Luc, the list of nominees held no surprises: Ella and Steve had nominated their respective spouses and Prince Ghazal nominated what could only be referred to as his most feminist wife or as he called her, 'The rebel in his harem'.

Wives and husbands were the obvious choices, demonstrating that even amongst the most eminent of politicians there still appeared to be a naive romantic view that one day far into the future on Mars, they may be paired up with their partners again. In reality this would be highly improbable, because the samples would be catalogued, numbered, and picked at random, if they were required at all. Gerry would also have nominated his wife but as she was no longer there, he went for the next obvious choice: nominating his secretary of state and closest friend Jenny Peters. She had given her entire life to politics and because of her dedication had never married or had children. Gerry had decided that possibly she should have a family, even if it *was* one she would know nothing about.

As for the Pope—well, in the absence of the Virgin Mary or Mother Theresa of Calcutta he had opted for his housekeeper, friend, and confidante Isobella Delle Grazie. She was a native Italian who had originally become friends with the Pope whilst he was at University in Rome and still just plain Richard.

How exactly Luc intended to acquire the DNA of those they had nominated would remain a mystery to everyone. Getting DNA samples from his guests had been easy enough: all he had to do was ask. However, they could safely assume that if Luc said he was going to do something then he was capable of doing it.

What they *did* know was that the rest of that year was not going to be easy for any of them. Ella James and Steve Cooper both had elections coming up. Steve Cooper considered it a bonus, using it to distract his attention from the asteroid. Unlike Ella he was not so concerned about his memory being erased, believing that there were certain advantages to living in ignorance.

Ella, on the other hand, couldn't see beyond the idea of intrusive brain surgery and the whole concept of it terrified her. She was determined to win another term in office, even if it meant abolishing local authority tax and giving every British citizen free booze, cigarettes, and petrol for the rest of their lives.

Prince Ghazal had to cope with the birth of his fourth baby son, knowing that he would be dead long before his life got the chance to start. It is always a tragedy when a child dies, but worse when that knowledge is there long before conception. He had always hoped that there would be no more children born in his family, and when one of his wives announced she was pregnant he was devastated. It was hard to believe Allah could be so cruel. He desperately hoped his belief in Luc wasn't misplaced but at the same time, he equally hoped it was.

Pope Gregory spent a lot of time with his head buried deep in the Bible along with various other less well-known documents. There are a lot of closely guarded secrets hidden within the Vatican and Pope Gregory was hoping Luc's identity was one of those secrets, or that at least there would be something to point him in the right direction. He knew there had to be more to Luc than met the eye.

The question was, how much more? Was he an Angel or a Demon?

Pope Gregory had a sneaking suspicion he may even be God but in order to be sure he needed proof. Hard evidence! The sort that comes in texts written thousands of years ago, by a host of different authors over several centuries.

The belief that Luc may be God was what enabled Richard to go along with the project. Surprisingly enough even the Vatican doesn't have the audacity to defy the will of its own God, at least not when directly addressed by God himself.

Unlike the others, Gerry had decided to award himself an easier time. He knew the asteroid was coming and he trusted Luc's advice that there was nothing he could do to stop it; this subsequently led him to the conclusion that there was no point in worrying about it. Therefore, as much as being President of the world's biggest superpower would allow, he divided his time between work and relaxation.

He allowed himself a certain amount of time each day to remember his wife and to grieve for his loss. He could easily console himself that although her death had been unpleasant he wouldn't have wanted her to stay alive just to face a more unpleasant ending a few years later. He felt a great deal of empathy towards Ghazal, but there was nothing he could do to make it any better. He also understood only too well Ella's neurosis about memory erasing; after all, he had gone through the same thing only a few months earlier. Even if he could find the magic words to make it all right, Luc's protocol did not allow for such direct communication amongst his guests.

Despite their own personal traumas none of them was prepared to betray Luc, least of all Pope Gregory. One Judas Iscariot is enough for any religion.

Fortunately for Ella, in May 2054 she successfully won another term in office, ensuring that her memory would remain intact. Watching the news, Gerry could see the relief on Ella's face. The press could make of it what they wanted; Gerry and the others knew her expression had nothing to do with the relief of winning an election or the end of a long, hard campaign but everything to do with keeping her memory.

The Australian election a few months later, was not so successful; at least, not in the conventional sense. Steve Cooper lost, but the news broadcasts revealed a man looking forward to a more relaxed lifestyle away from the pressures of the political arena.

Although they were all sorry to lose another person at Luc's table, it was only Ella who felt any real sense of loss. She knew that she would miss him at the next meeting and despite being happily married, spending time squabbling with Steve Cooper at Luc's was like having an affair without the need to actually have an affair.

Outside of Luc's, she had very little to do with the Aussie P.M., nor did she spend any real time thinking about him although that changed the day he was voted out of office. It took a few days for it to sink in properly and about another week before she felt able to call him. She felt an overwhelming sense of confusion as she dialled his number.

"G'day. Steve Cooper speaking."

'Now what?' she thought. There was a total feeling of uncertainty about her actions: she knew that she shouldn't really be phoning him, but she was desperate to find out if he still remembered her from Luc's. She was also fully aware that she could not directly mention Luc's name, which made the whole thing a bit awkward.

"Hello Steve, it's Ella … er … Ella James … from Britain … Prime Minister." She decided to stop there, aware that she sounded incredibly nervous and stupid.

"Yeah, I know who you are. I'm just wondering how you got this number."

"Oh … er …you gave it to me … Don't you remember?"

"No, not really, but okay, if you say so … Why are you phoning me anyway?"

She could tell that he was not only bemused, but also amused by the out-of-the-blue phone call. It was probably because the Prime Minister of England was sounding rather like a silly schoolgirl with a crush on him. That was something Steve Cooper would be likely to revel in at any time.

"I just wanted ... er ... to say ... I'm really sorry you lost your election."

"Well, it's very nice of you but I don't mind really; I've got plenty to keep me busy. I was a builder before I got into politics and Jeannie used to be a nurse, so we thought we'd see what help we could be in a few of the places that are still struggling from the effects of Yellowstone."

"Oh, well, okay ... Good luck then."

"Thanks. Well, if that's it I'd better go. I gotta lot to sort out."

"Yeah. Bye ... I'll miss you."

Ella pressed the button to end the call before he had a chance to reply. She knew he must think she had completely lost the plot, but at least she knew his memory *had* been erased. That had been the overall aim of the call. She had also told him that she would miss him and although it was said at lightning speed that was the other aim. There was absolutely no doubt in her mind that he had no idea why she had said it but knowing Steve Cooper, he probably assumed she really fancied him and was running around thinking he was some sort of sex god. It didn't matter what he thought: Ella had achieved her aims without betraying Luc; that was the main thing.

She also knew that it would be the last time she would ever speak to Steve Cooper.

CHAPTER 14

It was early in November 2054 when Luc's advert appeared in their local papers:

LUC IS HOSTING A PARTY
By invitation only
PO BOX 36369

This was the first time that Luc had used his name in public, and Gerry wasn't entirely sure that it *was* Luc. After all, it had always been made abundantly clear that his name was **never** to be used outside of their meetings. Yet here it was, bold as brass, right in the middle of the classifieds. There was also the possibility that it could be a hoax, written by someone who had *actually* managed to trace Luc. The worst-case scenario, as always, that terrorists were behind it.

It all seemed highly improbable, but nonetheless it was something that needed to be considered. After all, assuming that someone *had* tracked down Luc it was quite likely that they knew about the asteroid and, of course, the project. This sort of information would be more likely to have even the most fanatical of terrorists running around like headless chickens trying to figure out the best survival plan, instead of wasting their time and resources bombing cities that a few months later would cease to exist. Besides which, over the last decade the world had had far more important things to cope with and Luc had become a long-forgotten myth that had only ever been real to a very small handful of conspiracy theorists. Gerry was left with only one real conclusion: however strange this contact ad seemed it must be Luc himself. It didn't much matter, as either way he would still have to be ready for something. He just wasn't sure what.

Luc's world had always been strange: a world seen on the pages of Lewis Carroll or the canvas of Salvador Dali. Stranger still were Gerry's feelings as he prepared to go 'through the looking glass' for the last time: a cocktail of emotions that left him nauseous and unable to sleep.

Every now and then he would remember the strange advert and the swirling emotions would subside only to be replaced by fear; the same fear he had experienced the first time around. It is a strange world where a President not only hopes to find a stranger in their bathroom but would be relieved if they did. In fact, that was exactly what Gerry wanted, although it had to be a specific stranger: John.

Face to face with John in the bathroom, all fears of terrorists were rapidly dispelled. A calm sense of relief swept over him but was harshly snatched away when the Ghost appeared to collect him. He knew he didn't like the idea of this being their last meeting although it wasn't entirely clear to him which was the more distressing: not seeing Luc again or the end of the world. Either way, it didn't feel good.

As Gerry followed the Ghost, he remembered how nervous he had been the first time, back in the airport. He was still apprehensive, but it was different now: now he was aware that he would never get to know the old man as much as he would've liked. This was further reinforced by the knowledge that he was one of the few people who would know when the world would end.

He was still quietly considering the end of the world as the Ghost strapped him into the soft chair-bed aboard Luc's spacecraft. He thought about the countless documentaries he had watched that had speculated on how the world would end. Global disasters, such as Yellowstone, were hot favourites along with ice-ages, global warming, viruses, and of course, asteroids. He personally had always preferred the idea that one day, billions of years into the future, the sun would burn out leaving the Earth a cold, desolate planet. Of course, the inhabitants would have become advanced enough to leave the planet in search of a new world and obviously it would not affect a long-forgotten President McQuillan from the early 21st century.

A silence hung over them all as they entered the lift; a silence that was only broken when a smiling Luc welcomed his four remaining guests for the last time.

Gerry had no idea how long he actually spent at Luc's. He sensed it was probably longer than usual but for him it wasn't long enough and even when he did finally return to work he was still confused and unable to concentrate.

Gazing aimlessly around his office, he allowed the complex insanity of his life to wash over him. It only seemed a few hours ago that he had said goodbye to Luc for the last time and he was already beginning to feel a sense of deep, unfathomable loss. The sort of gap that no amount of kind words and well-meaning scriptures can ever fill. He knew that these things took time, but time was a luxury that he would never have again. The cold, numb sensation that slowly crept over him was not only due to the closing of that particular chapter of his life but came chillingly entwined with the knowledge that this next chapter was the final one. He wanted to reflect on his last meeting with Luc and, of course the others who, despite their prominence in the outside world were fairly insignificant next to Luc.

However hard he tried to remember it was all very hazy, appearing as little more than a disjointed dream. He knew they had spoken to Kabal via a satellite link or at least he presumed it was via satellite. He also knew that they were supposedly en route to Mars although he didn't really have the faintest idea when they had left, how far they'd got, or even when they were expected to land. That was how it was with most of the meeting: he had grasped the gist of it, but the finer points were missing. He did, however, have an uncomfortable feeling that he may have overdone it with his farewell speech to Kabal: perhaps one too many references to the pioneering spirit and he knew he'd thrown in a reference to the Alamo, but what he didn't know was why.

The only thing that could be considered any consolation was that although he didn't have any idea what Pope Gregory's speech was about (from his point of view it may just as well have been in Latin), it was at least longer than his and sounded more like it could have been a sermon rather than a farewell.

As for Ella and Prince Ghazal, he didn't remember them saying anything to Kabal. In fact, the only memory he had of Ella was her asking Luc if he would consider erasing her memory after all. This did seem very odd: Ella had always been so terrified of having her memory erased that it seemed very unlikely she would ask for it to be done. At the same time, it also seemed unlikely that Gerry had *imagined* her doing so. As it turned out, she *had* asked Luc to erase her memory; she hadn't intended to particularly but walking down the hallway she had spotted the blueprints of the sphinx that Steve Cooper had pointed out on their first visit. This was when it dawned on her that she missed him slightly more than she viewed as acceptable. After all, she loved her husband, and it was only the relationship she had had with Steve Cooper at Luc's that was making her feel this way. This led her to the conclusion that if she knew nothing of Luc and the time spent there, she wouldn't have any feelings for the Aussie. Ultimately, she would feel much less like an adulterous wife.

Unlike Luc, Gerry knew nothing of the bizarre train of thought that led to

Ella's request and Luc's agreement, so he remained unsure if he had dreamt it or not. He could only remember Ghazal speaking once, shortly before they left and that was to ask Luc for the impact date. It was information they had all wanted and Gerry now thought maybe he could have lived without it.

He didn't really understand what significance the phase of the moon or the vernal equinox had to do with it, although he had a horrible feeling that later on he might wish he had asked about it. He did, however, grasp the fact that it would appear in the skies around the 14th of March 2055 or as Luc put it, 'Give or take a day or two either way.' The impact date of the 21st of March 2055 at 09.01 GMT or 02.01 PDT was one of the few parts of the meeting he could honestly say he remembered clearly. After that, most of what was said appeared just as vague as it was before.

He was aware that Luc had proposed a toast to them; the exact wording of it eluded him but he had the impression it had been sincere and complimentary. The one sentence that Gerry remembered with true clarity came when they were entering the lift; this sentence he could recall every detail of. The others had gone ahead of him, and he was about to follow them when he heard Luc speak in a much quieter voice:

> *Dinonanistly altida caxvim,*
> *Lyvalciarint homus fratsch,*
> *Truledztu extravo,*
> *Novely extravol netx,*
> *Utgoesthulim Capriot vadum chexist"*

Gerry knew it was profound, he also had a pretty good idea that it was directed at him and only him. What he *didn't* know was what it meant. He assumed it was some flowery way Luc had found to say that they would always be friends, but he had no idea what language it was.

Once he was in the lift he wasn't the slightest bit interested in the others' discussion about how peculiar the wine tasted. He didn't care that it was sweet and sticky and not at all like the wine usually was, or whatever other comments they made about it. His wine had tasted the same as it normally did and for the moment, he was far more interested in what Luc had just said.

Now a very confused Gerry McQuillan sat in the familiar surroundings of his office still trying, if somewhat unsuccessfully to figure out exactly what Luc's comment was supposed to mean. He wasn't too sure how long he had sat there, but the arrival of Jenny for their habitual coffee morning brought him promptly back down to earth.

"Mmmm. Is now a good time to mention next year's Yelloween celebrations?" Still disorientated from his own thoughts, he was unable to properly decipher if it was a question or just a statement.

"What? ... Oh ... mmm."

His eyes followed hers to the large brown envelope on his desk that was clearly marked:

TENTH ANNIVERSARY YELLOWEEN

He remembered now. *That* was what he was *supposed* to be doing: going through the proposals for next year's Yelloween bash. He thought how much he hated the name *Yelloween*. It was such a stupid advertising gimmick.

"*Yelloween ...*" he pronounced with a look of total disgust, whilst simultaneously shaking his head and rolling his eyes.

"... What a stupid name."

"You really do hate it don't you? Well, I think it's fun ... kinda catchy. And we should commemorate the end of the eruption; the people are really looking forward to next year. Personally, I think we should make next year a really special occasion—push the boat out and mark the tenth anniversary of Yellowstone in style."

"Tell you what Jen. Seeing as you're so fond of this stuff why don't you decide what we do? Here's the proposals ... you choose which one."

"Well ... if you're sure?"

"I am. In fact, I'm sure you'll make a much better job of it than me. I used to always get Nina to do this sort of thing ... I mean ... I can't even wrap a present successfully ..."

"Yeah, I know." She laughed, forcing him to smile.

He didn't like the idea of letting anyone do all this work for nothing and certainly not Jenny, but he could see the excitement in her eyes at the thought of these celebrations and he had no right to take that away.

"It'll be really good, Gerry, I promise. Oh, yeah, and it won't interfere with work. I'll make it a ... personal project ... y'know ... like a hobby."

Around Jenny and her all-consuming optimism, Gerry couldn't help but feel better about life. However, once she had returned to her duties it didn't take long for him to sink back down.

He considered the idea that maybe he needed a hobby although what he really needed was for Luc to be wrong and failing that, less knowledge than he had. In truth, he was fast beginning to wish he had asked for his memory to be erased.

His thoughts swayed between wanting to share the burden with someone else and the guilt he would feel at betraying Luc, along with the dilemma of whether it was crueller to inform the public of their imminent destruction or to at least let them enjoy what time they had left. Realistically, whoever he tried to share it with would have rapidly had him removed from office and locked up. He felt sure of one thing: whichever decision he made the end result was going to be the same.

He even pictured himself at the next U.N. meeting, announcing how pointless arranging the next Yelloween celebrations would be as everyone would be dead by then because his imaginary friend said so. Of course, with the others to back him up they may be forced to listen, but even if they did there would be nothing they could do to alter it. There was always the option of admitting he was a raving alcoholic or drug addict, signing himself as unfit for office, disappearing into obscurity, and spending the rest of his days living on a diet of tranquilisers and beta blockers.

Not that it would prevent anything, it would just make it someone else's problem.

Eventually he managed to reason that the others must be going through the same feelings. Taking a deep breath, he made a pact with himself: if it ever got to the stage where he was unable to cope alone, then, and only then, he would get in touch with Ella, Ghazal, or the Pope. Like Luc said, if someone found him now then so be it.

As with all good ideas and resolutions this one was to be superseded by a better one, one that would help him to cope and better still, one that did not involve betraying Luc.

CHAPTER 15

Gerry McQuillan stood for quite a while just staring at the ground before finally speaking.

"I feel ... awkward ... not to mention a little stupid ... but I....well ... I really needed to talk to you. I feel very isolated and afraid ... I ... I don't really know where to begin. I s'pose just after Yellowstone. That's when I first met ..."

He paused for a moment, just to make sure no one else was listening before continuing:

"... I first met Luc." Gerry gradually stumbled his way through all his adventures, describing how he'd switched clothes with John at the airport and then later around Camp David. He talked about hologram Ghosts with their sci-fi ray guns, spaceships, and pleasant aromatic anesthetics. He explained how the children were housed in multi-layered facilities. Other topics included were Luc's house, Kabal, Layna, and the other guests. Eventually he concluded his monologue:

"So, you see, when I came back from Luc's the last time, I was unable to think clearly. I'm not sure how much of it is just that ... well ... I really miss seeing Luc. Obviously, I don't want the world to end.

Anyway, it probably sounds quite stupid ... but I made a pact with myself to call the others if it became too much. I'm not sure what I thought it would achieve but it ... well ... as it turned out, I didn't need to call them. I think knowing that I *could* was enough ... I don't even know what I would've said to them. Anyway, now I know that it would've done me no good as judging by the TV broadcasts of the Pope and Ella over the Christmas holiday, I believe neither of them can remember any of it. And I suspect that ... although ... well ... I do not know this for sure ... that Ghazal, too, has probably had his memory erased. I think it may have been something to do with the wine we drank at the last meeting, but I can't be sure of that either. I know it doesn't sound like I'm sure of very much, but I *am* sure that for the moment you are the only person I can tell all this.

At least I know that talking to you won't get me locked up ... I mean ... I'm not stupid and I'm not mad. I know exactly how insane this all sounds, but it's all true. I hope you can believe me ... I'm sorry ... I had better go now ... but I will come again ... Good-bye Nina ... I love you."

As he left his wife's graveside, he could see the security guards walking towards him. He knew he was right—Nina was the only person he could talk to; it was the only time he could feel safe in the knowledge that no one was listening in. Even security guards had to maintain a respectable distance at a graveyard; so far, even in 21st century America deceased wives were not yet considered a threat to national security.

As he left the graveyard, he felt the icy chill of the February air across his face. It made him feel alive, more alive than he had felt in a long time. Of course, he couldn't be too sure whether this feeling came from the cold weather or the fact that he had at last off-loaded some of the baggage he had been carrying around with him for the last few years. Either way it felt good, and an air of smugness crept over him as the magnitude of his achievement dawned on him.

For the first time he was aware that the odds against one man coping with all that was being thrown at him and remaining sane were absolutely astronomical. Yet despite those odds, Gerry was sane and, so far, he had told no one anything except of course his dead wife, who was hardly in a position to comment.

Regardless of how alive he was feeling at that moment in time he was still an older, burned-out version of the Gerry McQuillan who had first come to office back in 2052, and only he would be surprised by that which others had long seen coming.

CHAPTER 16

'Am I dead?' It was very bright, and his eyes appeared to be having difficulty focusing properly although he could see what appeared to be human shapes moving around him. They weren't very clear, but they were definitely there.

'Okay … I know it's not Luc's … the lighting's not right … perhaps it's the blast from the asteroid … maybe it's come early … oh God … I hope it's not … what else? … maybe they're not human … maybe they're aliens … they could be angels … oh God … I am dead.'

Realising his arms were by his side he pinched his right thigh – it hurt.

'Okay then, perhaps I'm not dead. So, where the hell am I?'

"Aah! Mr. President … good … I see you're awake now."

Now at least he knew that wherever he was they spoke the same language as him, which most likely ruled out aliens. As the figure got closer Gerry discovered that the reason, they had appeared so hazy wasn't a fault with his vision but, merely that in his half-asleep state, he had not realised there was a curtain around him.

"Where am I?" he mumbled weakly.

"You're in hospital, Mr. President. I'm Doctor Sabir."

"What's wrong with me? How long have I been here?"

"One thing at a time, Mr. President. You collapsed a week ago and you've been here ever since. As to what's wrong with you ... well ... I'm not sure. We ran a cat scan and there appears to be a foreign body in your cerebral cortex."

"What sort of foreign body? ... Like a tumor?"

"Well, that's just it; we don't know. It doesn't appear to be organic, nor for that matter does it appear to be anything obvious: like shrapnel or a bullet ..."

"So, what does it appear to be? And more importantly, what exactly is it doing to me?" Gerry was becoming increasingly agitated by their lack of knowledge. If there was a strange object floating around his brain, he wanted to know precisely what it was doing there.

"Like I said Mr. President, we don't know. I've never seen anything like it before ... take a look for yourself."

Gerry, who by now was completely awake, carefully looked at each of the scan images. The doctor was absolutely right: in the middle of his cerebral cortex was what looked like a small crystal pyramid. Gerry had no more idea than the doctor what the object was, but he suspected Luc was probably involved somewhere.

"I'd like to run more tests, if that's okay with you?"

Gerry thought for a moment. If Luc had put it there then there was probably a good reason why, and it may be better to leave well alone for the time being.

"What's today's date?"

"Erm, it's the 1st of March. Why?" Doctor Sabir appeared slightly irritated by the sudden change of subject, if not somewhat confused.

"Is there any other reason why I might have collapsed?" Gerry was running his own assessment on how dangerous this object may or may not be. It seemed highly unlikely that Luc would place an object in his head that would cause him any unnecessary problems. Luc's last cryptic message seemed to suggest that if he was likely to do anything, it would be painless and probably quick. It certainly wouldn't require him to become a laboratory rat for Doctor Sabir or any other doctor, for that matter.

"*Well* ... Your recent lifestyle is a possibility. I mean, judging by your appearance and overall well-being I would say you haven't been eating or sleeping properly ... not to mention some of the substances we found in your blood ...

However, I still feel the object in your brain may have played a larger part, and I would feel better if you would agree to us running more tests."

"Am I fit to return to work?"

"Well, yes ... but I'd give it a week or so ... just in case ... but really, Mr. President ..."

"Look!" Gerry cut him off in mid-sentence. He had no intention of letting any doctor near the object in his brain, but he knew he'd have to play ball with them in order to get back to work.

"If you agree to me returning to work next Monday, then I will come in for all the tests you want at the end of the month. I just have a few things to sort out first. Is that a deal?"

"Mmmm ... what if ..."

"Okay. Look ... if anything else happens to me ... well ... then you can do all the tests you want."

"Fair enough, Mr. President. It's a deal ... and you'll lay off the diazepam?"

"Doctor's orders, eh? ... Yeah, I'll lay off it." He knew the doctor was right about his lifestyle, but time had moved so quickly since New Year. Most people, he felt, would have turned to alcohol for emotional support during these difficult times, but for Gerry it was not an acceptable option as he had no wish to spend the last few weeks of his life as a drunken spectator. However, much he might want to pat himself on the back for not becoming a raving alcoholic, he wasn't a saint, nor had he spent the last few weeks being whiter than white.

He may not have turned to alcohol, but he had found other vices to help him cope:

Orexin for breakfast and diazepam for supper, with extra doses of either depending on whether he needed to stay awake or fall asleep. There was also the occasional pretty face to wake up to although, by comparison with other former Presidents Gerry was actually quite discreet about his activities. These vices were all easy enough for him to come by: like all Presidents, he too had friends in low places.

Regardless of how observant she was, Jenny had remained blissfully unaware of Gerry's socially unacceptable habits. That was, until he started smoking again. He quit tobacco twenty years ago but having decided that lung cancer was the least of his concerns he had returned to it with a vengeance.

Once aware of this habit she began to notice other things, like Gerry's overall state of health and how, both mentally and physically, he was going downhill fast.

Despite voicing her concerns quite graphically at times, Gerry continued with his somewhat unhealthy way of life.

Whatever his newly acquired vices were doing to him, they weren't helping him to forget the asteroid nor were they preventing the feeling of isolation he felt. In fact, all they had done was land him in hospital and while Orexin was a harmless non-addictive stimulant, diazepam was not. For that matter, neither was tobacco.

He may well have left the hospital drug-free, but staying that way was a bigger challenge. He had always been a strong-minded individual who would much rather be in control of something than have it control him. These days though it was much harder to keep control of his own mind, let alone anything else. Fortunately for Gerry his drug addiction managed to stay out of the papers, with the official line being, 'Suffering from Nervous Exhaustion.' This seemed far more acceptable than the truth.

In order to maintain any form of sanity he continued to visit Nina's grave. He was not a religious man, nor did he especially believe that there was an afterlife or that he was really talking to Nina but for whatever reason he found it comforting. It didn't matter that nobody else knew about the asteroid. He did. He also knew that his country needed him now more than ever before; as far as he was concerned, the people of America had chosen him to serve them. They trusted him and the very least he could do was do his best, and if standing in a freezing cold graveyard talking to a lump of stone kept him sane enough to do his job, so be it.

This plan worked relatively well, and a drug-free Gerry led the American people towards the end feeding them large helpings of apple pie and optimism. In fact, he did this remarkably well, right up until the night of the 13th of March. At this point the asteroid had still not become visible and while Gerry wanted to hope Luc might have been wrong, the feeling of impending doom as the end drew nearer was unfortunately now overriding any other emotions. Agitated and unable to sleep, Gerry caved in.

Armed with a large medicinal brandy and suffering from the worst delirium tremens since leaving the hospital, he headed to his dressing-room. Once there, he tried to visualize exactly which suit pocket he'd put it in. It took a while, but eventually he narrowed it down to a blue suit although he was unable to narrow it down any further than that. It took a while and after scrabbling through nearly every pocket he finally found what he was looking for: a bottle of diazepam and a packet of cigarettes.

By this time, he was shaking so much that just keeping hold of the bottle involved far more effort than he had initially expected. On top of trying to keep hold of the bottle, he was frantically trying to liberate the contents. This frenzied attack on an unsuspecting bottle of tranquilisers had only one inevitable outcome: minutes later there was an even more agitated Gerry McQuillan on his hands and knees, grasping a tablet off the floor.

No sooner had he grasped it than he had swallowed it. He sat on the dressing-room floor, with his back against the wardrobe. It had been exasperating, all that just to try and get some sleep. He toyed with the cigarette packet before eventually placing one in his mouth. At that point he realised he would have to move to get a light. Fortunately, that was a whole lot easier than the tablet fiasco as there was one on the dresser beside him.

Sitting back down on the floor he lit the cigarette and inhaled the deadly cocktail of tobacco, formaldehyde, arsenic, and other lethal chemicals. It tasted good. Better than that, it *felt* good. Holding it in his lungs for as long as he could, to get the maximum effect possible, he could honestly say no other cigarette had ever felt so good.

Looking at his watch it was 2:15 am but more to the point, it was the 14th of March. The diazepam didn't appear to be working, or certainly not as fast as Gerry would have liked it to. He discussed it with himself and decided to give it an hour before taking another one; he assumed that a couple more brandies might just do the job.

Eventually he passed out on the sofa in the living room, where he stayed until he was cruelly awoken by the phone ringing. He answered it without even bothering to open his eyes.

"Mr. President, you're needed immediately. We have a situation down here which requires your urgent attention."

He may have been half-asleep, but he knew exactly what their situation was.

"I'll be right there."

He sat up and rubbed his eyes. He thought he must still be dreaming, not because of the phone call though, without question that could only be the asteroid. It was because directly in front of him were two bare feet. Slowly, he allowed his eyes to work their way upwards assuming that either his eyes were deceiving him or the alcohol and tranquiliser combination he had ingested earlier was causing him to hallucinate. Whether he was hallucinating or not, the face looking back at him was unmistakable.

"Luc?" he whispered.

CHAPTER 17

"It's time for you to come with me now Gerry ... there's nothing else for you to do here."

"But the American people ... they need me."

"No, they don't." The tone in Luc's voice changed to one of sorrow as he stretched out his hand to Gerry.

"Look at you ... you have become worn down with the burden you carry. A burden that I placed on you and for which I am deeply sorry. You have always been a good President but now I feel it is time to call it a day ... there is nothing anyone can do now. Come on ... we will talk more later, but for now we must hurry ... we don't have much time. *Please, Gerry.*"

Gerry nodded. He was still unsure whether all this was, in fact, happening to him or if he was actually still asleep. For all he knew, it was nothing more than a substance-induced dream.

"Good ... now take off your socks."
"Why?"
"Don't ask questions, there isn't enough time ... I will explain everything later, but for the minute, *please* just do what I say."

Once again Gerry nodded compliantly.

"Okay. Now take my hand and whatever happens don't make a sound, all right?"

Taking hold of Luc's hand and still nodding like a dashboard ornament, Gerry slowly began to wake up.

As Luc led Gerry through the White House, he knew it was odd that nobody spoke to him or for that matter tried to stop him, but when was anything that involved Luc ever normal? Despite the peculiarity of the situation Gerry felt almost comfortable, as if he was going home for the first time in months.

He knew it shouldn't feel like that: as far as Gerry was concerned, no man should ever feel comfortable walking around in public, barefooted, whilst holding hands with another man. But this was different: for a start, they wouldn't normally be invisible to all those around them, which in this instance was a Godsend as there were rather a lot of very prominent politicians milling around who had all been called in for an emergency meeting with the President.

The only time Gerry felt any pangs of guilt was when he passed Jenny Peters on the stairs. She had always been a good friend to him, and it didn't seem fair that she would have to face this crisis alone.

These feelings however, had subsided by the time they reached the main doors. At this point any feelings of guilt were promptly replaced by a healthy fear of quite literally 'getting cold feet.' Despite all this Gerry dutifully followed along behind Luc, still holding his hand. It had become quite clear earlier on that somehow, holding Luc's hand was keeping Gerry invisible to those around him. Now it would also appear to be keeping his bare feet warm regardless of the actual air temperature, which Gerry knew could only be cold.

Outside, Gerry squinted. He knew that Luc's futuristic spacecraft must be around somewhere, but he couldn't see anything other than security lights and a continual stream of headlights as yet more politicians and diplomats arrived.

He felt an eerie shiver run down his spine as he continued to follow Luc through the grounds. Without question, anything that involved Luc, however interesting, was always strange but this was even more strange than usual. It may have been the hazy half-light that gave the White House gardens their Hollywood graveyard feel. It may also have been the emotional state of President Gerry

McQuillan as for the last time he walked through the familiar grounds of the place he had called home for thirteen years. It is, however, most likely that both these factors along with the valium and brandy binge he had indulged in earlier, had all contributed towards the Halloween effects he was now experiencing.

Gerry was so preoccupied with trying to get to grips with his current situation he hadn't noticed the slit opening in the side of the craft.

"We're safe now ... Gerry?"

"What? Oh ... Yeah." Gerry wasn't paying attention; he had stopped and was staring back towards the White House. There were so many memories housed within it ... Yellowstone, his wife, his friends, and work colleagues. There had been disasters and triumphs. All of which lived in there. It was impossible to accept that in seven days it would no longer exist.

"Shall we go?" Luc's voice was as soft and lyrical as ever.

"Okay." Gerry nodded, managing a weak smile.

Question after question raced through his mind but he knew it would be futile to ask anything at this moment in time, as Luc never answered anything until he was ready to. Besides which, the faint aromatic scent drifting through the craft meant that it was only a matter of minutes before he would be incapable of any conscious thought.

CHAPTER 18

"Gerry ... Wake up ... Luc's waiting for you."

Gerry opened his eyes, half expecting to find that it had all been a dream but the Ghost standing in front of him quickly dispelled that idea. He felt warm and safe and unlike the hospital, this time he knew exactly where he was. What he didn't know was how he got there.

"Uuh ... How did I get here? ... And where's Luc? ... And how long have I been here?"

"Oh, Gerry, you always ask so many questions ..." The Ghost sang in its usual reassuring tone. Hearing their voices was half the reason that he did ask so many questions: after all, he never got any proper answers from them.

"... I'm sure Luc will explain everything. Like I said before, he's waiting for you."

With that, the Ghost vanished. Gerry found that part quite disconcerting, not really expecting things to just vanish into thin air, at least not without any proper warning.

However, he was now in no doubt that he was back in Luc's world, where anything was possible, and everything was probable.

It was also quite apparent that the only way he was going to discover why he had been whisked away from the *real world* was to find Luc and ask him. It took him a while but eventually he made his way to the lounge. He was not entirely sure why he thought Luc would be there as opposed to any other room, but it did not come as any surprise to discover he was right.

"Hello, Gerry. It's good to see you again." Unfortunately, the serenity displayed by Luc wasn't quite enough to satisfy Gerry. It didn't much matter how pleased he was to see Luc again—at that moment in time he just needed answers.

"How long *was* I asleep for?"

Luc took a deep breath and, maintaining his serene composure, reiterated his opening comment. Gerry mellowed a little, considering the possibility that he may have been a touch ungracious towards his host.

"I'm sorry ... of course I'm pleased to see you again. I'm just a bit confused that's all ... I mean ... I'd expected to wake up on the aircraft ... not in a bed and certainly not without any idea how I got there ..."

"It's okay Gerry, I understand. Take a seat. We have much to talk about. And for the record, because you have been through so much I had the Ghosts bring you in to let you get some rest. And as to how long you have been asleep,... let me see ..." Gerry wasn't sure if it was his surroundings, the exceptionally comfortable sofa he had parked himself on, or just the sound of his host's voice but either way he felt a lot calmer.

"I reckon in linear terms about four days ... give or take a couple of hours."

"Four days!" he repeated, shaking his head. He could only assume that he must have been incredibly tired. Still, he was awake now and that's what mattered.

"Okay ... Well, I'd like to know why I'm here ... I mean, I didn't expect to see you again and it's not that I'm not pleased to see you ... it's just ... well ... that was what you said ... wasn't it?"

Luc smiled.

"You're here because I want you to be. I thought that as you are on your own ... and you have been through so much *more* than the others ... I thought it would be nice for you to escape the chaos and ..."

"And what?"

"Well ... face the end in surroundings that are a bit calmer."

"Oh ... I see. Well ... thank you ... I think ..."

"You think?"

"Well, I just thought ... okay ... I

know it's silly ... but I had kinda hoped ... well ... that you might be rescuing me. Still, I suppose it was a nice thought. Does that by any chance mean that you *did* erase the others' memories? I kinda thought you had ... was it something to do with the wine?"

Gerry was watching the expressions on Luc's face as he continued probing. Seeing that he was once again face to face with Luc he decided to make the most of the short amount of time there was left to get to know more about him.

"What made you think that it was the wine?"

"I don't know really. I s'pose ... if anything ... it may have been that they were all wittering on about it in the lift ... it tasted funny or something ... but mine tasted the same as it always did. Oh yeah, and that reminds me. What is that *thing* in my head? And *what* did you *say* as we were leaving? And incidentally, what language was it in?"

Luc smiled. The same smile that always came before one of Luc's obscure revelations.

"Okay, calm down Gerry. That *thing* as you put it is ... how can I explain this? It's ... in a nutshell ... it will help you to understand."

"Understand what exactly? Presumably not this conversation." For the first time in months Gerry felt like his old self. He had absolutely no idea what Luc was talking about, but he didn't mind. Of course, he had preferred his earlier idea of being rescued but even that didn't seem so important anymore.

"It would appear that you understood enough to not have it removed. Actually, it would have allowed you to understand my comment had you not been so full of chemicals ..."

Gerry toyed with the idea of trying to justify his behaviour by using sentences beginning with, 'Considering the circumstances ...' or 'I was under a lot of pressure ...' but thought better of it, knowing that no matter how good his argument might be Luc's would undoubtedly be better. Instead, he opted for remaining silent and looking shameful.

"... It is the eye of Horus ... a device invented by Horus ..."

"Woah! Woah!" barked Gerry, "Did you say Horus?"

"Yes."

"Like the Egyptian God?"

"Yes. The Egyptian God."

Gerry still looked baffled, and Luc could see that he was struggling with this particular gem of information.

"Look Gerry ... If you just accept there are many things that you do not know or as yet understand ... but if you let me finish I will explain everything."

Gerry nodded, not any the wiser but aware that he had just been told to shut up.

"As I was saying ... the eye of Horus ... commonly known as insight ... a device that allows you to see beyond the present. It can also show you the past and allow you to understand different languages and texts. In theory, when you have used it once you would be able to understand anything that was said to you or read and understand any text. This includes ancient and dead languages. Now, as I recall, my exact words were:

> "Dinonanistly altida caxvim,
> Lyvalciarint homus fratsch,
> Truledztu extravo,
> Novely extravol netx,
> Utgoesthulim,
> Capriot vadum chexist"

Which means exactly what it says:

> "Love is the highest power,
> The bond between true brothers,
> Slays all dragons,
> Even the dragon of death,
> As it is said,
> Therefore, it shall be."

"Which means *WHAT* exactly?"

"It means *exactly* what it says ... love is the highest power ... things which are done for the good or with the power of love are invariably more successful than that which is done through anger or malice. The bond that exists between true brothers ... or if you prefer, friends, ... is or at least *should be* love. Obviously, this love is different to sexual love ... far purer for a start and without the added distraction of lust. This pure, unconditional love slays all dragons or to put it simply, eases all pain. Lastly, it does not take away death, just the pain of death. This means that although I cannot prevent your death, I can however take away the pain."

"Oh, I see ... I *think* ... Well, thank you anyway ... but what about the last bit? You know ... the 'something or other shall it be' bit ..."

"As it is said. So, shall it be ... now I have said it, that is how it must be."

"Oh." Gerry was still not really any the wiser but decided not to pursue it any further, assuming that, like everything else it would hopefully become clear at some point.

"You still haven't told me what language it is ... or about the wine ... or come to think of it ... exactly why *I* need the eye of Horus."

"You're right. Firstly, you were absolutely right; it *was* the wine: it contained a neural anaesthesia, a sort of organic Trojan horse virus. I simply program the person to forget about me."

"Do they feel any *pain?*" asked Gerry, still somewhat sceptical that there was no pain attached to memory erasing.

"**No absolutely not!** Look Gerry, there is much that I want to share with you, but you must trust me. It is a very long time since I had anyone I felt comfortable enough to share things with ... for various reasons ... although lack of trust is usually the main one. Now tell me Gerry, do you trust me?" A sad far-away look came over his face; this was an expression Gerry had not seen before.

"Yes ... at least ... I think so ... I mean ... so far there's been no reason not to trust you ... *How long exactly Luc*?"

"*How long exactly* what?"

"You know ... since you trusted anyone?"

"Tell me Gerry, who do you think I am?"

"Luc?" responded an incredibly puzzled Gerry, "At least, I assume you're Luc. I know Richard thought you might have been an angel ... although ... I can't remember which one ... Gabriel ... maybe ...?"

Luc was grinning like a Cheshire cat, obviously finding the whole thing very entertaining.

"And you? Do you think I'm Gabriel?"

Gerry wasn't sure exactly what the right answer was and to be truthful, he had no idea who Luc was. Theoretically, he could be anyone, but as far as he was aware he was just Luc. To be perfectly honest, Gerry was too confused to be able to think properly and had opted for sipping a glass of water and saying very little.

"Well ... I didn't ... Why? Are you?"

"No, of course not. I'm Luc, always have been and always will be." For a moment there was silence as both men remembered **always** was only a few hours away. Gerry was the first to break the silence, determined not to let the asteroid get in the way of their last meeting. It would be there soon enough anyway.

"Well ... *actually* ... Luc, I did kinda wonder where you were from originally. I mean ... that thing you said ... what language is it?"

"Okay, Gerry. It's ... well ... it's ..." Luc paused just for a moment, and Gerry noticed that this was the first time that Luc had ever looked really uncomfortable.

Taking a deep breath and making direct eye contact with Gerry he slowly added,

"... it's ... Atlantean."

"You're from Atlantic City? But they don't speak like that in New Jersey."

"Not Atlantic City ... Atlantis."

"**What!?**" squawked Gerry, almost choking on the water he had been nervously sipping.

"Atlantis. Look, I know this is a lot to take in and I think it may be easier if I show you."

"Don't tell me we're going to Atlantis." Gerry was fast becoming unsure of anything; he was quickly losing the tenuous grip he had on reality as his conversation with Luc progressed.

"Not easily, as I'm sure you know it hasn't existed for thousands of years."

"Actually, I didn't think it existed at all ... it doesn't ... *Does* it?"

Luc got up and walked around to the back of the couch.

"I'll show you ... it'll be simpler. I need you to trust me as I have to blindfold you in order for the device in your head to work. Please ... just relax."

Gerry nodded compliantly. He had no idea where this was going but he couldn't think of any particular reason why he shouldn't trust Luc, besides he had nothing better to do.

He could hear Luc speak and felt sure he was saying something important, but Gerry was by now so deeply relaxed that only the information given to him via the eye of Horus could be properly focused upon.

Initially all that Gerry could see was darkness: a pure black nothingness, completely devoid of any physical form. Gradually a tiny speck appeared in the distance, which became a swirling ball of flames as it drew closer eventually increasing to a ring of fire that continued spinning and growing until only its outer edges were visible.

Within the centre of the ring images appeared: images from Luc's early life. He saw back to the time of Luc and his sister. Not in Atlantis, but in a research plant not unlike the ones where the children of the Martian project had been brought up. Except in this one, the children were branded at birth instead of getting the familiar birth certificate. He and his sister, it seemed, were bought by people from Atlantis which had to be the most prosperous place Gerry had ever seen. A small continent that had no poor or homeless people littering its streets. Every inch of it was magnificent with gold and marble buildings that shone in the bright sunlight. On the surface it seemed the perfect place to live, but as he continued to watch he realised there was a more sinister side to Atlantis. Although extremely prosperous, the people were also extremely vain and greedy who adopted children as symbols of wealth, rather than actually having any parental instinct. The women refused to have their own children as pregnancy and childbirth was not only painful but, more importantly, may ruin their perfect appearance. Luc and his sister were not anything like these people—wild and free-spirited children who loved the world around them but craved more from life than the shallow Atlanteans could offer. They were both extremely intelligent, beautiful children but their adoptive parents were unable to cope with these complex beings. Eventually, when they had exhausted all ways to make these maverick children fit into their society Luc and his sister were sold back to the research plant.

At that point Gerry saw the twists and turns that their lives had taken, including Luc's sister's marriage and her subsequent disappearance. He saw the people that Luc had encountered, leading up to the present day including the handful that Luc regarded as friends, and more importantly he saw why Luc was here and why he had chosen the countries he had to work with.

It turned out that rather than being related to money, land, power, or any of the usual diplomatic arse-kissing it was simply to do with old friendships from his early life. As he continued to watch Luc's life unravel before him, he learned more about the eye of Horus. He saw how, whilst it had a few prophetic abilities they were quite limited, allowing for more general predictions like those of Nostradamus and the Old Testament. He saw how it enabled people to think in a less conventional way, free from the constraints of linear time with more dimensions. As far as looking into someone's past or present was concerned, that always required their consent.

One thing Gerry saw was the truth behind Luc's incredible spacecraft. Gerry had always been fascinated by this and it had come as a bit of a let-down to discover that rather than using plutonium, krypton, anti-gravity, or warp-drives they were, in fact, controlled by telepathy as were most things in Luc's world. This particular revelation made it easy for him to understand how Kabal and the children could travel to Mars so quickly. In fact, they actually intended to leave the Earth's atmosphere just as the asteroid entered it. The method in this madness was to preoccupy Kabal's mind with powering the craft so he was unable to dwell too much on what was happening to Luc. There was so much to take in but all in all, it gave him a much greater insight into why the current asteroid situation was one event that was beyond Luc's control.

In those last moments Luc had shown Gerry many things, most of which were beyond comprehension: like not only where Luc was from, but where he currently lived, and his true age.

Gerry did not feel in the slightest bit afraid. If anything, he felt an even greater sense of trust for Luc than he had before.

As soon as the blindfold was removed Luc began to speak,

"… of course, there was a device made once that had no limits …"

"What?" whined Gerry, unable to really take in what Luc was saying.

"Eye of Horus. There was one made once that allowed the user to see into someone's past and their entire future just by thinking about them. Needless to say, there was only ever *one* made …"

"Do *you* have that device?"

"**Me**? … Absolutely not! It's a dangerous piece of equipment … that sort of thing could send you over the edge. Can you imagine being able to see into the hearts and minds of all humankind … how paranoid would you become?"

"I s'pose so, but I still get the feeling you know who does, or at least who *did*, have it ..."

"Not for sure ... but I could probably hazard a good guess. Still, it doesn't much matter now, does it?"

"Mmm ... That's a point ... how long *have* we got left?" Gerry had managed to forget about the asteroid until Luc had reminded him.

"Does it matter?"

Gerry knew it didn't and just shook his head, almost grateful that Luc had not told him the precise number of hours and minutes until his death. Luc reached out and taking both of his hands, quietly whispered to Gerry,

"Do not be afraid, my friend. All is as it should be."

Gerry did not feel the slightest bit afraid. If anything, he felt an even greater sense of trust for Luc than he had before.

Still holding both Gerry's hands Luc knelt before him, bowing his head, and tipping it slightly to one side to reveal his birth tattoo.

"See, Gerry ... Let him that hath insight, let him calculate the number of the beast, for it is a man's number. His number is six hundred three score and six."

At that moment, a sublime knowledge crept over him. The knowledge that he had always existed and would always continue to exist. A sensation that somehow made death appear to lose its sting and in many ways, he was as ready to embrace it as it was to embrace him.

It was not long before the first hint of the fragrant anaesthesia could be detected, and a deeply relaxed President Gerry McQuillan surrendered himself willingly in the knowledge that ... All was ... As it should be.

CHAPTER 19

The upshot of Gerry's mysterious disappearance had meant that Vice President Kyle Samuels had suddenly become President Kyle Samuels who along with the rest of the world leaders, had been reliably informed that while the asteroid was likely to cause substantial problems it would be unlikely that it would be responsible for the total extinction of the human race. Experts conceded that whilst an asteroid of similar size may well have brought about the sudden demise of the dinosaurs, they also graciously pointed out that on the whole humans were generally cleverer and somewhat more resourceful than their reptilian predecessors.

The biggest question mark was not over the diameter but the shape. How could an asteroid this small possibly have enough gravity to be a perfect sphere? Along with the fact that despite their attempts to nuke it, with the intention of either nudging it out of the way or blasting it into smaller and hopefully less destructive fragments, the asteroid remained not only intact but also on course.

This meant the newly appointed President and the rest of the world leaders were left to make their own provisions to ensure the maximum survival rate. This entailed a range of ideas including lotteries and privately selecting candidates from more eminent members of the population, to doing nothing at all and hoping people found their own survival methods.

Within seven days, exactly as Luc had predicted and at the appointed time the asteroid barged its way through the atmosphere on a direct collision course with the South Pole.

Within seconds the breath-taking icescape that for millions of years had so magnificently gilded Antarctica was instantly evaporated as the glowing sphere embedded itself deep within the icy continent, triggering a chain-reaction of unrestrained chaos. In the dark skies, which only hours before had shone so elegantly with the stylised hues of the polar sunset an intense fireball raged, scorching the land for miles around. Mount Erebus, Deception Island, and several other submarine volcanoes were resurrected by the impact whilst the Antarctic plate that had been stable for so long began to move, causing the already weakened plates to rupture, thus initiating a series of earthquakes and volcanic eruptions.

The sheer devastation continued to escalate as shockwave after shockwave spanned the globe. The oceans boiled as hot magma spewed out from the fractured seabed. Every eschatology myth ever conceived was coming true. People could put down their placards prophesying the second coming, end of the world, or whatever doom and gloom they were peddling. *It was happening.* For those who had long awaited a glorious 'Second Coming' of their Lord this must have been a bitter disappointment, a far cry from the paradise they had so long awaited.

Within an hour of the asteroid entering the Earth's atmosphere humankind was almost a thing of the past.

As for the handful who had survived in their 'protect them from everything' underground bunkers, they only really had a limited amount of time left. As soon as they were forced up to the surface, hungry and diminished in numbers raging fires, acid rain, a toxic atmosphere, and certain death would be all that greeted them.

Far away and in a peaceful contrast to the raging inferno that, only yesterday they had called home, Kabal and the colonists watched the sublime beauty of their first Martian sunset. Blue streaks filled the dusky pink skies as the sun inched its way below the horizon, while in the distance a glowing red star could be seen in place of a once-fertile blue planet.

For the children who had been brought up in secret facilities buried deep below the surface of the Earth, it was the beginning of a new life. A life of freedom and wonder. Not only were they the last remnants of the human race they were also the forefathers of a new race.

However, for Kabal and Layna it was a harsh reminder of those they had left behind. More accurately it was a harsh reminder of Luc. The loss Kabal felt was immeasurable; the void left by the loss of this man he had loved as if he were his own father could never be filled. Kabal knew he was never fully going to understand why Luc had chosen to remain on Earth any more than he understood why Luc had chosen to spend the last few hours of his life with Gerry McQuillan. Only Luc could answer these questions, but he was no longer around to ask. The knowledge that at least Luc had not died alone was of little, if any, consolation to Kabal: as far as he was concerned Luc should be there on Mars with him.

Many times, Kabal had recollected the last conversation he had with Luc. He could not totally recall exactly what he had said to Luc, but he knew it was along the lines of why Luc wanted to remain on a dying planet when the new world was a project to which he had dedicated so much of his life.

Nonetheless, he could clearly remember every detail of Luc's face as he smiled before delivering his well-thought-out response:

"Mars is a place for young blood, not old bones ... I have known from the beginning that my place would be here at the end. It is also my choice and although you don't understand it, I expect you to respect it. Moreover, I expect you to be a far better teacher than I would be. And, for that matter, a better example."

There was a tear in Luc's eye as he hugged Kabal and whispered, "Make me proud, son. Make me proud."

Now stood on the surface of their new home watching the sun go down, Kabal resolved to do just that. He would be someone that Luc would be proud of.

Printed in the UK
by
clocbookprint.co.uk